"Who are you with today?" asked The Great Sybil.

"My friend Caitlin. We're looking at the exhibits and going on the rides and . . ." Ellen stopped. "My brother came, too," she said. "Corey."

"Your younger brother? A small boy?" asked the fortune teller.

"He's nine. He came with his friend Nicholas, and his friend's mom."

"Perhaps there is danger ahead for Corey."

Despite the warm room, Ellen shivered slightly. She remembered her mother saying, "Trouble always comes in threes."

"I advise you to keep a close watch on Corey for a few days."

Ellen thought, that'll be a switch; usually he spies on me. Aloud she said, "I'll try."

"Good. The spirits occasionally use automatic writing when they have an urgent message to communicate," The Great Sybil said. "It is not wise to ignore the spirits."

"What spirits?" Ellen asked. "Who sent this message?"

～

"A gripping sequel to *Terror at the Zoo* and *Horror at the Haunted House*."   —*School Library Journal*

BOOKS BY PEG KEHRET

DANGER
AT THE FAIR

PEG KEHRET

PUFFIN BOOKS

PUFFIN BOOKS
Published by the Penguin Group
Penguin Putnam Books for Young Readers,
345 Hudson Street, New York, New York 10014, U.S.A.
Penguin Books Ltd, 80 Strand, London WC2R ORL, England
Penguin Books Australia Ltd, Ringwood, Victoria, Australia
Penguin Books Canada Ltd, 10 Alcorn Avenue, Toronto, Ontario, Canada M4V 3B2
Penguin Books (N.Z.) Ltd, 182-190 Wairau Road, Auckland 10, New Zealand

Penguin Books Ltd, Registered Offices: Harmondsworth, Middlesex, England

First published in the United States of America by Cobblehill Books, an affiliate of
Dutton Children's Books, a division of Penguin Books USA, Inc., 1995
Published by Pocket Books, a division of Simon & Schuster Inc., 1997
Published by Puffin Books,
a division of Penguin Putnam Books for Young Readers, 2002

1 3 5 7 9 10 8 6 4 2

THE LIBRARY OF CONGRESS HAS CATALOGED THE COBBLEHILL EDITION AS FOLLOWS:
Kehret, Peg.
Danger at the fair / Peg Kehret.
p. cm.
Summary: Ellen receives a spirit message during a séance at the county fair, warning
that her brother Corey is in danger and that she must rescue him.
ISBN 0-525-65182-9
[1. Fairs—Fiction. 2. Extrasensory perception—Fiction. 3. Criminals—Fiction.
4. Brothers and sisters—Fiction.]
I. Title.
PZ7.K2518Dan 1995 [Fic]—dc20 94-16873 CIP AC

Puffin Books ISBN 0-14-230222-8
Printed in the United States of America

PROLOGUE

ELLEN STREATER stared into the darkness as the hall clock struck twelve.

Midnight. The perfect time for ghosts and spirits, she thought. If he's ever going to hear me, it will be now.

She sat up and swung her legs over the side of the bed, searching with her toes for her slippers. Silently, she moved to her dresser, feeling along the top until her hand closed over the small silver elephant.

It was the first time she had intentionally touched the elephant since the night of the accident. Then, overcome with rage and grief, she had unfastened the chain and flung the elephant into the wastebasket. "You didn't bring good luck," she had said. "You brought terrible, horrible luck."

The next day, someone—Ellen assumed it had been her mother—retrieved the elephant and put it on Ellen's dresser. It had lain there all these months, growing dusty, a reminder of the worst day of her life.

1

It was not what Grandpa had intended, when he gave it to her.

"I know how much you like the elephants," he had told her, "and an elephant with its trunk curled up is a symbol of good luck. When you wear this, you'll remember our fun trips to the zoo."

It had been a special gift, chosen especially for her. Now, as she stood in the midnight blackness, Ellen hoped the silver elephant might somehow help her make the connection she longed for. More than anything, she wanted her words to be heard and understood.

Cupping the elephant and its slender silver chain in her left hand, she held it close to her heart and whispered, "Grandpa? Wherever your spirit is, I hope you can hear me. I want to tell you what happened today. Maybe you already know. Maybe you were part of it."

She paused briefly, wondering where to begin. With the strange message? With the Tunnel of Terror? With the realization that someone wanted to kill her?

Ellen took a deep breath, squeezed the silver elephant, and began with breakfast that morning.

CHAPTER

• 1 •

"HERE COMES The Gruesome Green Ghoul!" Corey Streater, with his arms above his head and his fingers spread like claws, lurched into the kitchen.

His sister, Ellen, took another bite of toast and ignored him.

"Eat your breakfast, Corey," Mrs. Streater said, "or you won't be ready to go to the fair when Nicholas and Mrs. Warren get here."

"I'm ready now," Corey declared. "I'll eat breakfast at the fair, as soon as I ride the Tilt-a-Whirl and The River of Fear."

"You'll eat breakfast right here," Mrs. Streater said. "It's probably the only decent food you'll get all day."

"The Gruesome Green Ghoul eats people," Corey said. He grabbed Ellen's arm and pretended to take bites from her wrist to her elbow, as if her arm was corn on the cob.

Ellen jerked her arm away, glad that she was going to the fair with Caitlin and would not have to put up with her little brother's nonsense. "I wouldn't go on that River of Fear ride if you paid me," Ellen said.

"Is that the big enclosed ride that stays on the fairgrounds year-round?" Mrs. Streater asked.

"That's the one," Ellen said. "Some kids that rode it last year told me it's the scariest ride they were ever on."

"Good," Corey said, as he spread peanut butter on a slice of toast. "When I grow up," he continued, "I'm going to invent The Gruesome Green Ghoul ride and I'll go to all the fairs and run it and pretend to eat people."

"*If* you ever grow up," Ellen said.

"My ride will fly upside down and rotate in circles and whip back and forth, all at the same time, and you'll have to ride it standing on your head with bare feet. You'll get strapped down so you don't fall off and there'll be this huge green blob, like a giant amoeba, that bites at your toes and then . . ."

"Don't expect me to ride on it," Ellen said.

"The Gruesome Green Ghoul ride will be the scariest ride ever invented," Corey said. "Even scarier than The River of Fear. I'll make a trillion zillion dollars, and spend it all on corn dogs."

"You forgot to take the bandage off your face," Mrs. Streater said.

"I didn't forget," Corey said. "I like it. It's the best Batman bandage I ever saw. I'm going to wear it for a whole year." He took a drink of orange juice and then screamed as loudly as he could.

Ellen dropped her toast.

"What's wrong?" cried Mrs. Streater.

"Just practicing," Corey said. "I plan to go on every ride and I'm going to scream and scream and scream."

"Don't overdo it," Mrs. Streater said. "You're still hoarse from that throat infection. If you scream all day, you'll lose your voice altogether."

"Hallelujah!" said Ellen.

A horn beeped in front of the Streaters' house.

"It's Nicholas!" Corey yelled. "I'm leaving!"

"Good," said Ellen.

"Be careful," Mrs. Streater said. "Stay with Mrs. Warren and do exactly what she tells you."

Corey dashed out the door.

His mother called after him, "Don't eat too much junk!" but Corey did not hear her. He was lurching toward the Warrens' car, shouting, "Here comes The Gruesome Green Ghoul."

Mrs. Streater poured herself a cup of coffee and sank into a chair opposite Ellen. "Did you ever notice," she said, "how quiet it seems right after Corey leaves?"

Ellen laughed.

"I hope he behaves himself," Mrs. Streater said. "Fairs and carnivals can attract some rather seedy characters and you know how Corey is, always imagining that he's a spy and other people are dangerous criminals."

"Mrs. Warren will watch him."

Mrs. Streater nodded. "Yes. Your father says I worry too much. But trouble always comes in threes, you know, and I can't help wondering what the third will be."

A terrible windstorm in January had uprooted a fir tree and sent it crashing across the Streaters' garage, causing extensive damage. Then, in March, they lost Grandpa. Ellen thought no trouble could be as bad as that and she knew from the sad look on her mother's face that Mrs. Streater was thinking the same thing.

A dark sense of foreboding swept through the sunny kitchen, pushing aside the warmth of the August morning. Quickly, Ellen finished her toast and carried her dishes to the sink. Trouble coming in threes is nothing more than an old superstition, she told herself. What could be more safe than the county fair?

❖ ❖ ❖

"DON'T VOLUNTEER any information," Mitch Lagrange told his wife, as they waited to cross the border from Canada to the United States. "Answer questions pleasantly but don't say anything more."

"I'm not stupid," Joan Lagrange replied.

Mitch looked in the rearview mirror at his nine-year-old stepson, Alan. "You pretend to be asleep," he said.

Mitch pulled the car up to the enclosure where the border guard sat.

"Where do you live?" the guard asked.

"Seattle."

"How long were you in Canada?"

"Overnight."

The guard looked around Mitch and addressed the next question to Joan. "What did you do there?"

"We took my son to the Vancouver Aquarium." She pointed to the back seat, where Alan lay with his eyes closed.

The border guard nodded and waved them on their way.

"I knew they wouldn't have a stolen vehicle report yet," Mitch said. "I doubt the owner has even realized the car is missing. Still, it's a relief to get across the border without any problem."

"Portland, here we come," Joan said, "to collect our ten thousand smackeroos."

Mitch stayed just under the speed limit as he drove south on Interstate 5. "I wish I could open it up," he said, "and see how fast this beauty will go."

"When you're driving a stolen Mercedes with counterfeit license plates," Joan replied, "you don't take chances."

"This handles like a dream," Mitch said. "It's a shame to strip it and sell the parts."

"We'll get twice as much for the parts as we would for the car," Joan said, "so don't get any funny ideas." She consulted the map of Washington State. "The turnoff for the fair in Monroe is Highway 2," she said. "But do we *have* to waste a day visiting your brother? If we keep going, we'll be in Portland in time for lunch. The fair is fifteen miles out of our way." She looked at the map again. "Monroe doesn't even rate a red circle on the map. It's only a tiny black dot, like a period."

"I owe it to Tucker, to see how he's doing."

"You don't owe him anything."

"We should have posted bail when he asked us," Mitch said.

"We didn't have an extra three thousand dollars sitting around."

"We could have come up with it, if we had tried." Mitch exited the freeway and headed east on Highway 2. "It's been hard on Tucker the last six months, working for a carnival in order to stay on the move after he jumped bail."

"It wasn't our fault he got caught faking car accidents so people could turn in false claims to their insurance companies. Why should we have to bail him out?"

7

Half an hour later, Mitch handed two dollars to the parking lot attendant and pulled the Mercedes into the line of parked cars at the fair.

"There's a Ferris wheel," Alan said, "and a big roller coaster. This is going to be fun."

"Let's work the fair, Mitch," Joan said.

"Are you crazy?"

"It would be like old times, picking pockets for a living."

"No, thanks," Mitch said. "What if we got caught?"

"We won't get caught. And even if we did, we'd be let off with a warning or a small fine. A little country fair, way out in the boonies like this, won't have a decent police department. They probably can't even check fingerprints or get computer data."

At the mention of fingerprints, Mitch stiffened. His greatest fear was to have his fingerprints checked, although Joan didn't know that. He had never told his wife about his past; she thought he had always been Mitch Lagrange and Mitch saw no reason to enlighten her. Joan could never tell someone else what she didn't know herself.

"I used to outsmart them in Los Angeles and San Diego," Joan continued. "We won't get caught here."

"Maybe not, but why stick our necks out when we don't need the money? We'll make ten grand on this car deal and it's a sure thing, with no risk now that we've made it across the border."

"We need a little excitement," Joan said. "The car business is boring."

"Bor-ring," echoed Alan.

"Good," Mitch said. "Boring means no trouble."

8

"We could cut Tucker in on the day's take. We'll find a way for him to help and give him fifteen or twenty percent."

"I'll help," Alan offered, "if you give me twenty percent, too."

Joan laughed.

"Please, Mitch?" Alan said. *"Please?"*

"People bring money to a fair," Joan said. "We could help them get rid of it."

Mitch shook his head.

She gave him that odd narrow-eyed look, the one that always made him wonder if she suspected he had concealed his past when they married last year. As if to confirm what he was thinking, Joan said, "Don't be so paranoid. Sometimes you act as if you're wanted by the feds. All we want to do is pick a few pockets."

"I'll bet my *real* dad would do it," Alan said.

Mitch sighed. He hated it when Alan said things like that when Mitch tried so hard to be a good father.

"My *real* dad isn't chicken," Alan said.

Mitch wanted to say, "Your real dad is a fool who spends more time behind bars than free." Instead he said, "Oh, all right. We'll try it for awhile."

CHAPTER

◦ 2 ◦

THE DARK gold lettering gleamed in the afternoon sun:

FORTUNES TOLD.   PALMS READ!
SEE INTO YOUR FUTURE
What Message Will the Spirits Have for You?

Ellen and her friend Caitlin stood beside the Ferris wheel at the fair and read the writing on the side of the large trailer. Painted ferns, flowers, and rainbows surrounded the words and a trio of angels, painted in pink, gold and white, hovered above the message. Across the bottom, in smaller letters, it said:

The Great Sybil Sees All, Knows All
Two dollars admission.

"Let's do it," Ellen said. "Let's have our fortunes told."

"No way. I'm not wasting two dollars on some fake in a turban who pretends to see things in a crystal ball."

"It would be fun," Ellen said. "She might tell you there's a handsome stranger in your future."

Caitlin ate a handful of popcorn. "The only thing I want to know about my future is whether or not I'll make Drill Team and I doubt if any carnival gypsy knows that."

"I'm going to do it," Ellen said. "I've always wanted to have my fortune told." She took two dollars out of her wallet.

Caitlin frowned. "What if she sees something bad in your future? Would you want to know?"

Ellen hesitated.

"Oh, forget I said that," Caitlin said. "The Great what's-her-name won't pretend to see anything bad. It wouldn't be good for business."

"What do you mean, *pretend*?" Ellen said, acting shocked. "The Great Sybil sees all and knows all; it says so right here." She grinned at Caitlin.

"If I want to listen to someone who sees all and knows all," Caitlin said, "I can hear my mom, for free."

Ellen gave her money to the bored-looking man who sat in a small ticket booth at the entrance to the fortune-teller's trailer.

"Go right in," he said. "The Great Sybil waits to enlighten you."

Caitlin, rolling her eyes, whispered, "The Great Fake waits to bamboozle you."

Despite Caitlin's cynicism, Ellen eagerly opened the door and stepped inside. She expected a dark, gloomy room, with heavy draperies, glowing candles, and possibly incense burn-

11

ing. Instead, the trailer was filled with greenery. Plants of all kinds grew in large redwood tubs and brass pots. Tendrils of ivy climbed the walls, crossed the ceiling, and descended the other side, intertwined like braids. Bright red blossoms covered a large cactuslike plant and a hint of rose petals filled the air. Ellen felt as if she stood in a jungle or an exotic greenhouse.

"Welcome." A tall woman, her black hair tied back with a green ribbon, stepped from behind a huge philodendron. Despite the warm day, she wore a fringed shawl over her blouse, and a long green skirt. She carried a large tin watering can. "I am The Great Sybil. And you are?"

"Ellen. Ellen Streater."

"Ellen. Wise and understanding, like a light in the dark."

"Excuse me?"

"Your name. Ellen. It comes from the Greek, Helene, meaning, 'A woman whose wisdom and understanding are like a light in the dark.' "

"I didn't know that." Ellen wanted to write that down, so she could tell Caitlin the exact words, but it seemed awkward to take out a notebook and start writing in the middle of a conversation, as if she were a newspaper reporter.

Ellen looked around. A small couch, covered in dark brown velvet, snuggled under a gigantic fern. Two straight wooden chairs, with a small bare table between them, stood in the center of the room. She wondered if she should sit down.

"Names are important," the woman said. "When a person is given the right name, it helps to shape that person's destiny."

"What does your name mean?" Ellen asked.

The woman looked surprised, as if no one had ever asked that before. "Sybil is Greek, also. It means 'prophetess.' "

"That fits. Did your parents name you that or did you choose the name when you started your fortune-telling business?"

"My name has always been Sybil," the woman said sternly, as if Ellen had insulted her.

"Oh. I thought it might be a business name, the way authors sometimes use a pen name."

"No. Sit, please." The Great Sybil gestured in the direction of the table and chairs. She put the watering can on the floor.

Ellen sat on one of the chairs, keeping her hands in her lap where they were hidden by the table. Trying not to be too obvious, she opened her shoulder bag, took out a small notebook and pencil, and wrote, "Helene: wise and understanding. Light in the dark."

After dimming the lights, The Great Sybil sat across the table from Ellen. "Do you have any special concerns?" she asked. "Is there something in your future that worries you?"

"No. I just thought it would be fun to have my fortune told."

"There is a blue aura about you," The Great Sybil said, "which indicates you are good at communication. Perhaps we will be able to get a message for you from the spirits."

"Spirits?" Ellen said. "What spirits?"

"The beings who live among us, unseen."

Ellen said nothing.

"You look doubtful," The Great Sybil said. "Most people willingly accept that other beings may live in outer space. So why not here? If spirits can exist on Mars or Jupiter or in between and beyond, why can't they exist here on Earth, as well? Just because we can't see them doesn't mean they aren't here. We don't see television transmissions, either, but we turn on our sets, confident that there will be a picture."

13

Maybe Caitlin was right, Ellen thought. Maybe I shouldn't be doing this.

The Great Sybil smiled at her. "Do not be nervous," she said. "The spirits are kind and loving. There is nothing to fear. Close your eyes, please."

Ellen did.

"Breathe deeply. Relax."

Ellen took a deep breath and then another, feeling the tension ease out of her shoulders.

"That's right. Clear your mind. Think only of the sky and the clouds and the sunshine. Open your heart to whatever message the spirits might have for you today."

The woman's voice was low and soothing. Ellen tilted her head back slightly as she imagined blue sky and clouds like fat cauliflowers overhead.

"Loving spirits," said The Great Sybil, "come to us today. Look down on your friend, Ellen, who seeks wisdom and understanding."

Behind her closed eyes, Ellen imagined a gathering of angels, like the three painted on The Great Sybil's trailer, floating over the fairgrounds toward them.

"Oh, spirits," droned The Great Sybil. "We give you our love and friendship. What message do you have for Ellen today?"

The trailer was still. None of the sounds of the midway seeped through. Ellen, feeling half-asleep, waited.

"Ellen is ready, spirits," whispered The Great Sybil. "Ellen is open to receive her message."

Whack!!

Ellen's hands jerked upward and slammed the notebook onto the tabletop. Her right hand stiffened on the pencil and

14

the pencil raced across the paper. Startled, Ellen opened her eyes and stared at her hands. The pencil moved rapidly across the notebook page but Ellen had no idea what she was writing. She tried to stop writing but the pencil continued its hectic scribbling. It was as if her hand belonged to someone else.

When the notebook slammed onto the table, The Great Sybil opened her eyes, too. Ellen heard her draw in her breath, as if in astonishment.

It lasted only a few moments. Then, as suddenly as it had begun, the pencil stopped writing and Ellen's hand relaxed.

"What happened?" Ellen said.

"What did you write?" The Great Sybil asked.

"I didn't write anything. I mean, I don't know what I wrote." She squinted at the paper but in the dim light she could not make out the words. "The pencil just started moving and I couldn't do anything about it. It was as if my hand belonged to someone from outer space and wasn't connected to my brain at all."

She stopped. Maybe this was a prearranged trick, something that happened to everyone who paid to have their fortunes told. Yet, the woman looked genuinely surprised.

The Great Sybil put her hands on the table and, leaning toward Ellen, whispered, "So. You are one of the gifted ones."

Ellen said nothing. If this was all a show, the fortune-teller was a terrific actress.

The Great Sybil flung her arms wide, as if to embrace the entire room. "Thank you, spirits," she said. Her vibrant voice sounded tinged with awe. Clearly, she had not expected this to happen. "Ellen and I thank you for your kindness."

Ellen's pulse pounded in her throat.

The Great Sybil said, "You have received a wonderful gift,

15

Ellen. In all my years of fortune-telling, this has never happened before. You are able to open the channels of communication between this plane of existence and the next. The spirits can speak through you."

Ellen felt goose bumps rise on her arms.

The Great Sybil's eyes glowed; her excitement filled the room. "Let us read the message the spirits sent you." She rose and turned the lights brighter.

Ellen looked at the piece of paper. "It isn't my handwriting," she said. "The words lean backwards, the way a left-handed person's writing sometimes does."

"Of course, it wouldn't be your handwriting," The Great Sybil said. "*You* wrote nothing. One of the spirits wrote the message, using your hand—your body—as a tool. It's called automatic writing; psychics can sometimes do it."

"I'm not a psychic," Ellen said.

"Many people have talents of which they are not aware. What does your message say?"

Ellen looked at the paper again. At the top of the page in her own, round script, it said, "Helene: wise and understanding. Light in the dark." Below those words, in the odd slanted script, was the message.

Ellen read aloud: *It is for you to know that the smaller one faces great danger. He will pay for his mistake. It is for you to know that the paths of destiny can be changed and the smaller one will need your help to change his. You will know when it is time. Do not ignore this warning.*

She finished reading aloud and then quickly read the message again, to herself.

"May I see it?" The Great Sybil asked.

Ellen's hand shook slightly as she tore the slip of paper from

16

the notebook and handed it to The Great Sybil. "What does it mean?" she asked.

"Is there a young child in your care?"

"No."

"Do you do baby-sitting, perhaps?"

"I baby-sit for my neighbors sometimes but they have two little girls. The message is about a boy."

"Who are you with today?"

"My friend Caitlin. We're looking at the exhibits and going on the rides and . . ." Ellen stopped. "My brother came, too," she said. "Corey."

"Your younger brother? A small boy?"

"He's nine. He came with his friend Nicholas, and his friend's mom."

"Perhaps there is danger ahead for Corey."

Despite the warm room, Ellen shivered slightly. She remembered her mother saying, "Trouble always comes in threes."

"I advise you to keep a close watch on Corey for a few days."

Ellen thought, that'll be a switch; usually he spies on me. Aloud she said, "I'll try."

"Good. The spirits occasionally use automatic writing when they have an urgent message to communicate," The Great Sybil said. "It is not wise to ignore the spirits."

"What spirits?" Ellen asked. "Who sent this message?"

"I don't know that. Your guardian angel, perhaps, or a spirit who loves you, or one who loves the small person who will be in danger. The important thing is not who sent the message; it is what you do about it. You have been offered a chance to change the small one's destiny. Perhaps, even, to save his life."

"But the message is so indefinite. I don't know for sure who

17

the small one is or what the danger is or when it's going to happen. How can I help someone when I'm not even sure who I'm supposed to help?"

The Great Sybil gave the paper back to Ellen, pointing at the line that said, *You will know when it is time.* "You will know when it is time," she said. "Trust the spirits."

"I would be more trusting if I knew who the message was from."

The Great Sybil said, "Have you lost a loved one recently? Someone who would feel close to you, even though they are no longer with you?"

Grandpa.

The word exploded in Ellen's brain, sending fragments of fresh grief through her entire body. Her eyes swam with tears.

"You have," The Great Sybil said.

Ellen nodded. "Grandpa," she whispered.

"Perhaps your message is from him."

Ellen stared at the woman. Was it possible? Could the odd warning somehow be a message from Grandpa?

"Sometimes a loved one who has recently gone on tries to contact those who are left behind, to let them know that he or she still exists. In your case, perhaps your grandfather sees a danger that could be avoided and he wants to help."

Images flashed through Ellen's mind: the look on Dad's face when he told her and Corey that a drunk driver had hit Grandpa's car; Grandma crying at the memorial service; the hollow feeling Ellen got when she saw Grandpa's favorite chair, forever empty. She was not yet used to having him gone; the idea that his spirit might have written her a note was more than she could face.

Snatching the piece of paper from the table, Ellen sprang to

18

her feet. Caitlin was right; she should not have come here.

"Wait!" said The Great Sybil, as Ellen rushed out the door. "We must talk further."

Brushing tears from her cheeks, Ellen stumbled down the trailer's steps.

The Great Sybil called after her, "Please come back! I can help you. We'll do another reading, for no charge."

Ignoring the woman's words and the startled man in the ticket booth, Ellen ran away from the trailer.

CHAPTER

❖ 3 ❖

THE FERRIS WHEEL stopped with Corey and Nicholas in the top bucket. "Hi, clouds!" yelled Corey. "Hi, sun! Look at us: we're on top of the world!"

He leaned forward to look down on the fairgrounds, causing the bucket to sway. Nicholas gripped the bar and pressed his back stiffly against the seat.

Below the Ferris wheel, crowds of people moved in all directions, eating, talking, enjoying the fair. "Maybe I'll see Ellen down there," Corey said. He turned sideways and looked over, causing the bucket to sway even more.

"Sit still," said Nicholas.

Corey craned his neck, searching in all directions for a glimpse of his sister. She was always too wimpy to go on the Ferris wheel and he wanted her to see him way up here in the sky, like a bird. He tucked his hands in his armpits and flapped his elbows up and down, like wings. "I'm a woodpecker," he said. "No, I'm an eagle, flying to my nest."

"Hold still," said Nicholas.

"Nicholas, look!" Corey stopped flapping and started to stand up as he pointed over the edge of the bucket. Nicholas grabbed Corey's shirt and yanked him back down.

"That man stole a purse!" Corey cried. "He took it out of a baby stroller." Corey's voice rose and he talked faster in his excitement. "I saw him! Look! There he goes! The woman must have left her purse in the stroller basket and that man with the shopping bag helped himself and he put her purse in his bag and now he's going to get away. She doesn't even know he did it."

Details, Corey reminded himself. Good witnesses have specific details. He tried to see what it said on the man's shopping bag but the man was too far away.

Corey waved both hands over his head and yelled at the man who ran the Ferris wheel. "Bring us down! Hurry!!"

Nicholas had heard Corey tell wild stories too many times to believe him without questioning what Corey said. "The man was probably the woman's husband," Nicholas said. "Maybe he's going to buy their lunch."

"He isn't. He's a thief. I'll bet there are police and F.B.I. agents all over the fair, looking for him."

The Ferris wheel began to turn but it stopped again with Corey and Nicholas in the nine o'clock position. Corey still hung over the edge of the basket. "He's getting away," he said. "He's clear over there now, by the stand that sells pineapple on a stick. He went in that big building." He waved at the Ferris wheel operator again. "Hurry!" he shouted. "We have to get off! We have to catch a criminal."

The basket finally stopped at the bottom and the attendant pulled back the bar so Corey and Nicholas could get off.

"Why didn't you bring us down sooner?" Corey demanded. "Couldn't you hear me yelling?"

"You and thirty others." The operator turned to an older couple who stood in line to get on the Ferris wheel. "Kids," he mumbled. "They can't wait to get on a ride and then they can't wait to get off."

"Maybe that woman is a wealthy princess and there were millions and millions of dollars in her purse," said Corey, as he and Nicholas went through the exit gate for the Ferris wheel ride. "Maybe she's a rich movie star or a famous singer. When we identify the thief, she'll probably give us a big reward and we'll go on every ride six times and have money left over."

The boys went toward where Corey had seen the man take the purse. A group of people crowded around a woman who held a toddler. She was talking to a uniformed fair security guard.

"I left it in the stroller while I put Jennie on the little car ride," the woman said, "and when I came back, it was gone. All my money! All my credit cards!" She started to cry. "Even my driver's license!" Seeing her mother in tears, the toddler began to cry, too.

"Are you a princess or a movie star?" Corey asked. "Did you have millions of dollars in your purse?"

"Are you kidding?" sniffed the woman.

"Run along, son," said the guard.

"I saw the man who took the purse," Corey said. "I was on top of the Ferris wheel and I saw him do it." Corey talked faster and faster, his eyes round with excitement. "He was carrying a big shopping bag and he put the purse in the bag and then he left. Maybe he is a dangerous criminal. Maybe he's wanted by the F.B.I. and we'll be famous for catching him and we'll get our picture in the paper."

"Can you describe the man?" the guard asked.

Corey tried to remember. He was sure he would recognize the man if he saw him again but it was hard to describe him. "He was kind of average looking," Corey said.

"What was he wearing?"

"Pants. And a shirt. They were both dark colored." He knew his description was too vague but no matter how hard he tried, he couldn't recall anything unusual about the man, except the shopping bag. "He carried a big white bag," Corey said, "with red and blue lettering." He beamed at the guard, certain that the shopping bag was the perfect clue.

"Like that one?" The security guard pointed.

Corey looked. A man walking past carried a white paper shopping bag that said MADE IN THE U.S.A. in red and blue letters.

"Yes!" Corey said. "Exactly like that." He looked closely at the man. "That isn't him, though," he said, "but maybe it's his partner. Sometimes criminals work in pairs. You had better talk to that man quick, before he gets away. Look in his bag and see if the purse . . ."

The guard interrupted. "One of the commercial exhibitors gives those bags away," he said. "There are probably two hundred people walking around today carrying bags exactly like that."

"There's another one," Nicholas said, pointing at a woman.

"Oh," said Corey.

The guard took a small notebook from his shirt pocket, wrote down a phone number, and handed the paper to Corey.

"If you think of anything that would help identify the thief," he said, "please call this number."

Corey nodded and put the paper in his pocket. Phooey. For a moment, he had thought he would be a hero. He could almost see the newspaper headline: LOCAL BOY FOILS THIEF!! And, under the headline, a picture of Corey, accepting a reward from the grateful woman after she got her purse back.

"Be alert," Corey said, as he and Nicholas walked away. "We might see him again."

"I didn't see him the first time," Nicholas said.

◇ ◇ ◇

CAITLIN waved from a shady bench near the Tilt-a-Whirl ride. Ellen sank down on the bench beside her.

"So, how was it?" Caitlin said. "Did you find out if I made Drill Team? Do you know who you're going to marry? Did you learn if you'll be rich or . . ." she stopped talking and put her hand on Ellen's arm. "Ellen?" she said. "Are you OK? You're white as a snowman." She looked closer. "You've been crying."

"I got a warning," Ellen said.

"She gave you bad news?"

"The Great Sybil didn't. I got a message from the spirits."

"What kind of a message?"

"It's a warning that something bad is going to happen, probably to Corey. I think the message is from—from Grandpa."

"But your Grandpa . . ." Caitlin clamped her lips together. "We ought to complain to the Fair Board," she said. "That fortune-teller has no right to upset you this way, pretending she can talk to the dead."

"She wasn't pretending. Oh, Caitlin, it was so strange."

"I'm sure it was. Strange and well-rehearsed. Those people are all phonies; you know that, as well as I do."

Ellen shook her head. "It wasn't fake," she said. "The Great Sybil was just as shocked as I was."

"Oh, sure." Caitlin patted Ellen's arm. "I know you miss your grandpa," she said. "It's been real hard for you since his accident, but you have to be realistic, Ellen. If that woman really could communicate with people who have died, she wouldn't be traveling around in a tacky painted trailer, charging two bucks to read fortunes. You notice there's no long line of people waiting for her to enlighten them."

Ellen looked down at her hands. She knew Caitlin made sense, yet she couldn't shake a sense of misgiving.

"If your grandpa's spirit could send a message," Caitlin said gently, "why wouldn't he have sent it to your grandma, or to your mom?"

"Maybe I'm the only one who can communicate. Remember when I worked in the Historical Society's haunted house and the ghost of Lydia Clayton spoke to me and nobody else could hear or see her?"

"That was different. You were in Lydia's former home and she had a problem that she needed your help with."

"This time, Corey has the problem and Grandpa—or some other spirit—is trying to help."

"If it's true that you are the one who can communicate, you would not need The Great Sybil as an intermediary. The spirits could talk directly to you." Caitlin lowered her voice. "If your grandpa's spirit wanted to tell you something, I don't think he would whisper in your ear when you're at the fair. He would do it when you were home alone and could pay close attention."

Caitlin stood up. "Forget about The Great Sybil. She's nothing but a phony and your so-called message is only a trick. Let's go pig out on cotton candy."

Ellen stood, too. How could she explain what had happened in that plant-filled room? Caitlin had not been there. She didn't witness Ellen's pencil darting across the paper as if it were alive. She didn't see the look of excitement on The Great Sybil's face or hear the awe in her voice.

As Ellen followed Caitlin toward the cotton-candy stand, she put her hand in the pocket of her jeans and touched the piece of paper. She wished she could believe that Caitlin was right and the warning was merely a trick. It would be much easier to laugh it off, as if it were a silly message in a fortune cookie.

But what if it was real?

What if Corey was destined for some terrible danger?

And what if Grandpa was trying to warn her?

CHAPTER

• 4 •

"WHAT HAPPENED? That girl was crying." The bored man came out of the ticket booth and approached The Great Sybil, who stood in the trailer's open doorway.

"She had a message from the spirits."

"Oh, sure. What did you tell her, Sybil? You have to be careful with kids that age. Get them all upset and they run to their parents and you'll end up with the State Attorney General's office closing us down."

"I didn't tell her anything. It was a real message."

"Are you serious?" The man stepped inside the trailer and closed the door behind him. "What happened?"

"She was holding a pencil and a notebook and the spirits did automatic writing."

"Holey-moley." The man slumped into one of the chairs. "How long has it been, thirteen years? Fourteen?"

"Fifteen. When I started charging for my services, the spirits quit coming. Fifteen long years ago."

"Fifteen years since you actually had any communication, and then it happens with some hysterical kid who can't handle it."

"She wasn't hysterical. She got a warning and then, when I asked if she had recently lost a loved one, it hit a nerve. Apparently, her grandfather died not long ago."

"Oh, great. She's going to run home crying and tell Mama that she talked to Grandpa, who died last week. The cops should be here any minute. Geez, Sybil, you need to be more careful."

"Careful! How was I to know this would happen? I was just as surprised as the girl was when that pencil started to move." The Great Sybil sat opposite the man, put her elbows on the table, and leaned her chin on her hands. "It was glorious, Willie," she said. "It was just the way it used to be, when I still had my talent."

"Why?" he said. "Why now, after all these years, are you suddenly able to do it again?"

"I can't. The girl can."

"You led her into it, didn't you? You got her relaxed and called the spirits to come?"

"Yes. But they didn't come to me, they came to her. I was merely a spectator."

"She paid her two dollars, just like everyone else. She bought a ticket before she went in." Willie frowned. "You've always said you lost the talent after you started charging money to do readings. You said the spirits quit coming because it was a business for profit, not a true spiritual search."

"The girl, Ellen, made no profit. Her search was genuine."

"What do you plan to do if the girl's parents show up, angry because you misled their daughter and upset her?"

"I didn't mislead her! If anyone asks, I'll tell them the truth. She got a message."

Willie shook his head. "The truth is, you've hoaxed people out of their money for fifteen years. Now, I'm the first to admit I encouraged you. When you first lost your talent, I told you to fake it and who would know the difference? The way I see it, if people want to spend their money, we'd be foolish not to take it. Still, it's hard to believe that after fifteen years of hoaxes, you are suddenly the witness to a real message from the spirits."

"It's been more than a hoax, all these years," The Great Sybil said. "I've made a lot of people happy because of the 'messages' they got. They've come in here anxious and upset and I've sent them away calm and optimistic. Is that so terrible?"

"You tell them what they want to hear," Willie said, "whether it's true or not."

"This time, I didn't. I swear it, Willie. This time, the spirits spoke. If anyone asks, that's what I plan to tell them."

"Well, it makes me nervous," Willie said. "If any more kids want to buy tickets, I'm going to say they have to be eighteen or older in order to get in."

❖   ❖   ❖

"THE MESSAGE wasn't whispered in my ear," Ellen told Caitlin. "It was written on my notebook paper, by my pencil, held in my hand."

The two girls sat in the top row of the arena where Caitlin's

29

cousin was scheduled to show his sheep. They were early, so it was a quiet place to talk.

Ellen handed Caitlin the message and watched Caitlin's expression change from scorn to concern as she read it.

"That is scary," Caitlin said, as she handed the paper back to Ellen. "It is definitely not your handwriting and I don't see how it could be a trick, either. Not when it was your own pencil and you were holding it."

"It doesn't look like Grandpa's handwriting, either," Ellen said. "But who else would the message be from?"

"Maybe it's from your guardian angel."

"That's what The Great Sybil said. I didn't know you believed in angels."

"My aunt says everyone has a guardian angel," Caitlin said. "She prays to hers every day, asking the angel to keep her safe."

"Sort of like a fairy godmother?"

"Not exactly. Aunt Catherine says we each have an angel who is always with us, to guide us and help us. Sometimes, when we think we have a good idea, it's really our angel who puts the idea into our head. Aunt Catherine even asks *her* angel to talk to other people's angels. When we went on our vacation last year, she had her angel ask my angel to be especially watchful over me while I was away from home."

"Does she ever get written messages from her angel?"

"No," Caitlin admitted, "but I suppose all angels are different. When I was little, I used to imagine that my guardian angel sat on top of my bookshelf at night, watching me sleep, and shooing away any goblins. It was comforting."

"You never told me this before."

"It isn't the sort of thing that comes up in ordinary con-

30

versation. I always wanted to think Aunt Catherine was right, but it's been a long time since I believed there was an angel on my bookshelf."

"Whoever it is from," Ellen said, "the message makes me nervous."

"What are you going to do about it?" Caitlin asked.

Ellen shrugged. "What *can* I do?"

"Are you going to tell your parents?"

"No. Mom would get upset and Dad would say The Great Sybil is a fake and tell me never to go back."

"What about Corey? Will you tell him?"

"I don't know. I don't want to worry him and I'm afraid if I tell him, he'll blab to my folks. You know what a motormouth he is."

Caitlin nodded. "Still, if he's going to be in danger, maybe you should try to warn him. He might be more cautious."

Ellen looked again at the slip of paper in her hand. "The danger is some time in the future," she said. "I don't think I'll say anything to Corey just yet."

"Maybe you'll get another message," Caitlin said.

"What do you mean?"

"Well, *you* did the automatic writing, not The Great Sybil. Maybe you can get messages from the spirits any time you want."

Ellen did not answer. What if Caitlin was right? What if she could contact—contact who? She was not at all sure she wanted to receive more messages from the dead. Not even Grandpa.

❖ ❖ ❖

COREY raised his arms high above his head, aimed at the red spot in the middle of the stack of wooden milk bottles, and threw the ball as hard as he could. Thunk! It hit almost in the center of the spot, toppling six of the bottles. The remaining four bottles wavered for an instant but remained upright.

"Phooey!" said Corey.

"Sorry, son," said the man who ran the bottle-throw booth. "Care to try again?" As he spoke, he picked up the fallen bottles and restacked them.

Corey dug into his pocket for three more quarters. Even though he thought seventy-five cents was way too much money just for a chance to throw a ball at a stack of wooden milk bottles, Corey was determined to win one of the stuffed dinosaurs that hung from the ceiling of the booth.

"You aren't doing it again, are you?" asked Nicholas. "You've already lost four times." He finished his corn dog and wiped the mustard from his mouth with his sleeve.

"I want that Tyrannosaurus."

"It would be cheaper to go to the toy store and buy one."

Corey wished Nicholas wouldn't be so practical. It spoiled Corey's grand dream of telling everyone how he won the giant stuffed dinosaur at the fair. Won it! For free! Just by throwing a ball and knocking over some wooden milk bottles.

"Win a dinosaur!" yelled the man, as a group of boys approached the booth. "Only seventy-five cents to win one of these giant, authentic, stuffed dinosaurs."

"Let's go ride the roller coaster," Nicholas said.

"I'm going to try one more time," Corey said. He plunked his money on the counter. The man quickly swept it into his apron pocket and handed Corey another ball.

Corey licked his lips and rubbed the ball between his hands. Using his best Little League pitching form, he flung the ball toward the stack of bottles. This time, the ball hit exactly where he aimed, square in the middle of the red spot. The top three bottles flew off and all of the bottom bottles except one toppled immediately. That one rocked back and forth so violently that the top of the bottle hit the floor before it straightened again. Then it rocked slower and slower until it finally stopped in an upright position.

"Sorry, son," said the man. "Care to try again?"

"I hit the spot!" Corey said. "I hit right in the middle."

"Must have been a shade to one side," said the man.

"It wasn't! I hit dead center!"

"Win a dinosaur!!" yelled the man, covering up Corey's voice. "Step right up and try your luck. Only seventy-five cents for a genuine, authentic stuffed dinosaur."

"I should have won, shouldn't I, Nicholas? That ball hit right smack where it was supposed to."

"I wasn't watching," Nicholas admitted. "Just as you threw it, that kid tripped and dropped his ice-cream cone and I got distracted." Nicholas pointed to where a woman comforted a crying boy. A chocolate ice-cream cone lay in the sawdust at the boy's feet.

A man standing near the boy said, "Don't cry, little boy. I'll give you some money to buy another ice-cream cone." He reached toward his back pants pocket and then began frantically searching all of his pockets. "It's gone," he said. "My wallet is gone."

Corey and Nicholas looked at each other in surprise. "Another robbery?" Corey said.

CHAPTER

· 5 ·

COREY LOOKED around for the man with the shopping bag but did not see him. A group of curious people now surrounded the crying child, his mother, and the frantic man.

"I had my wallet when I bought my ticket to get in," the man said to no one in particular, "and I got it out to use my telephone credit card awhile ago."

"You probably left your wallet in the phone booth," suggested the woman with the little boy. "I did that once."

"Maybe it's still there," the man said. He hurried away.

"Let's go ride the roller coaster," Nicholas said.

"That bottle guy is cheating," Corey said. "One of those bottles is rigged so it won't fall over no matter where the ball hits. We ought to spy on that man and see how he does it and report him to the Fair Board. I bet nobody ever wins a dinosaur. Those same dinosaurs have probably been hanging there for a million years."

"That's why he calls them authentic," said Nicholas. "If we're going to ride the roller coaster before my mom comes back, we'd better get going."

Corey shoved his hands in his pockets and stomped away from the bottle-throw booth. He *did* want to ride the roller coaster and he knew that if he and Nicholas waited until Nicholas's mother was with them, she might say no. Mrs. Warren had allowed the boys to go off on their own while she went to the flower exhibit only after they promised to stay together and to meet her in exactly one hour. She did not make them promise not to go on any scary rides but they both knew it was only because she hadn't thought of it.

In addition to the Ferris wheel, they had already ridden The Giant Lobster Claw and the Tilt-a-Whirl. Corey screamed so much on The Giant Lobster Claw that his throat hurt but he didn't mind. Half the fun of going on a scary ride was being able to scream as loudly as possible. If there was a prize for Best Screamer at the Fair, Corey was certain he would win it.

While they waited in line for the roller coaster, they ate strawberry ice-cream cones and looked across the midway toward The River of Fear. A wooden stairway led to a platform that was as high as the top of the Ferris wheel. People climbed the stairs and waited on the platform to begin the ride.

"The River of Fear ride is working again," Corey said. Earlier, there had been a rope at the bottom of the stairs, with a CLOSED sign hanging from it.

A recorded spiel boomed from speakers at the top of the platform: "Experience a death-defying descent down Whiplash Waterfall! Travel through the Tunnel of Terror! Meet the monsters of Mutilation Mountain! Are you brave enough to ride

35

The River of Fear? YES!! Astonish your friends! Climb the platform now and begin the journey of a lifetime. RIDE THE RIVER OF FEAR!!"

"After we do the roller coaster," Corey said, "let's ride The River of Fear."

"My mom will have a heart attack if she sees us up there."

"She'll have a heart attack if she sees us on the roller coaster, too."

"True. She still wants me to ride the little fire trucks in kiddieland."

Corey laughed. He knew Nicholas was exaggerating but he also knew Mrs. Warren would never allow the boys to go on anything as exciting and dangerous-sounding as The River of Fear ride. Since The River of Fear was enclosed, it was impossible to tell, without going on it, exactly how scary it was. For Corey, that was part of the appeal.

The boys got in the roller coaster car, buckled the safety strap, and pulled the metal bar forward. As the car climbed, swooped, climbed again, turned, and plunged toward the ground, Corey closed his eyes and screamed and screamed and screamed. This was great! Ellen could probably hear him screaming clear across the fairgrounds.

When the ride ended, he turned to Nicholas and tried to say, "Let's do it again," but he was so hoarse the words didn't come out. Maybe his mother was right; he should not have screamed quite so much.

One look at Nicholas told him that Nicholas wouldn't want to ride again, anyway. All the color had drained out of Nicholas's face and he had one hand clamped over his mouth.

Corey climbed out of the car. When Nicholas started to stand, he swayed and sat down again, resting his head on the metal bar. Corey helped Nicholas out of the ride. Nicholas walked bent over, holding his stomach. There was a small picnic area nearby and Nicholas staggered to one of the picnic tables, sat on a bench, and leaned his head on his arms.

A stand selling curly fries stood next to the picnic area. Corey sniffed the air and decided to buy some. He loved to dip the spirals of deep-fat-fried potatoes into catsup and eat them.

He carried the heaping container of curly fries to the picnic table, along with a paper cup filled with catsup.

Nicholas still had his head down. Corey nudged him. When Nicholas looked up, Corey held out the curly fries and croaked, "Want some?"

Nicholas looked as if Corey had offered him poison. He shook his head violently and turned the other way, so he couldn't see Corey eat.

Corey munched the curly fries, hoping Nicholas would feel better soon. He also hoped his voice would come back before they rode The River of Fear. It wouldn't be as much fun to be scared if he couldn't scream.

"There you are." Nicholas's mother approached the picnic table. When she reached the boys, she put her hand on Nicholas's forehead. "You're sick, aren't you!" It was a statement, not a question. "You probably ate too many of those fatty French fries."

"No, he didn't," whispered Corey. "All he ate was a corn dog, a bag of taffy, two scones, some onion rings, a Polish sausage, and an ice-cream cone."

"Ohhh," said Nicholas, as if it made him sicker to hear the words.

"Your voice!" cried Mrs. Warren. "Corey, what happened to your voice?"

Corey tried to say, "I think I screamed too much," but even the whisper was gone now. His words were much too faint for anyone to hear. He pointed at the roller coaster.

"You went on the *roller coaster*?"

Nicholas groaned again and Corey realized he should not have pointed.

"Well, it's small wonder you're sick, Nicholas," his mother said. "I thought you had more sense than to ride on a roller coaster. It's a miracle you're alive to tell about it. We're going straight home and put you in bed."

To Corey's surprise, Nicholas did not argue. He nodded meekly, as if bed sounded good to him.

Corey poked Nicholas's arm and then pointed at The River of Fear. Nicholas shook his head and put his hand over his mouth again.

Phooey. What rotten luck for Nicholas to get sick before they could go on the best ride of all.

"Come along, Corey," said Mrs. Warren.

"I'll ride home with Ellen," Corey wheezed.

"What's that? I can't hear a word," said Mrs. Warren.

Corey pointed to himself and mouthed the words, "My sister."

"I think he wants to stay here and go home with Ellen and Caitlin," Nicholas said.

Corey nodded vigorously.

"I can't leave you here by yourself," Mrs. Warren said. "Where is your sister?"

Corey dropped to his hands and knees at Mrs. Warren's feet.

"Good heavens," said Mrs. Warren.

Corey mouthed the words, "Baa, baa."

Mrs. Warren looked at him, blinking nervously.

"Caitlin's cousin shows sheep for 4-H," Nicholas said. "Maybe Ellen is in the sheep barn or the show arena."

Corey nodded again.

"We go past the 4-H buildings on our way out of the fair," Mrs. Warren said. "If your sister is there, we'll ask if you can stay with her."

She took Nicholas by the arm and led him away from the midway. Corey trailed behind, eating his curly fries. As they passed the bottle-throw booth, he saw a group of girls, each buying a turn to throw. He wanted to shout, "Save your money! That guy cheats!" but without a voice, all he could do was feel sorry for the girls.

When they reached the 4-H complex, Mrs. Warren said, "We'll look in the show arena but if your sister isn't there, we can't traipse all around hunting for her."

Corey was relieved to see Ellen and Caitlin sitting in the top row of the show arena. Corey nudged Mrs. Warren and pointed at the girls. Mrs. Warren waved at Ellen.

Ellen waved back.

"What happened to your brother's face?" Caitlin asked.

"He got cut when he fell off the monkey bars at the park," Ellen said. "It's healed now except for a scab across his cheek but he insists on wearing that stupid Batman bandage."

"Nicholas and I will wait here," Mrs. Warren said, "while you go up and ask Ellen if it's all right for you to stay and go home with her."

Before Corey could do so, Nicholas bolted toward one of the trash cans that stood just inside the door. He leaned into the trash can and threw up. Mrs. Warren handed him a tissue to wipe his mouth, then turned to Corey. "Stay with your sister," she said.

"I will."

Mrs. Warren put her arm around Nicholas and pushed open the door.

Corey wished Nicholas wasn't sick. It wouldn't be half as much fun to scream on the scary rides alone. Ellen never wanted to ride anything except the merry-go-round. He sighed and turned toward the steps to join Ellen and Caitlin.

"Sorry," said a voice at his elbow. "No food is allowed in the stands."

Corey went outside to finish his curly fries. As he emerged, he heard someone crying loudly. Looking toward the noise, he saw the same boy who had been near the bottle-throw booth. Once again, the boy was crying and pointing at an ice-cream cone on the ground while his mother tried to calm him. That kid, thought Corey, should buy ice cream in a cup and eat it with a spoon.

"Hey!!"

Corey looked at the gray-haired man who had shouted.

"Someone took my wallet!" the man yelled. "Everyone stay where you are! Call the police!"

Corey could hardly believe his ears. *Another* pickpocket? He quickly scanned the crowd of people, most of whom reacted to the man's shouts by clutching their own wallets and purses.

There he was!

The man in the dark shirt with the MADE IN THE U.S.A. shopping bag was easing past the people who had stopped to stare at the shouter.

Corey tried to yell, "That's him! He's the thief!" but he

could not make a sound. Corey watched as the man moved quickly through the crowd, shaking his head at the other people as if to say, *How terrible*.

Corey couldn't let the man get away. Forgetting his promise to stay with Ellen, he took off across the fairgrounds after the thief.

CHAPTER

◦ 6 ◦

"I'm going to go talk to The Great Sybil again," Ellen said.

"Now?" said Caitlin. "The 4-H kids are bringing their sheep in. We'll miss Ben."

"You can stay and watch the sheep show. I'll come back here when I'm finished."

"Are you sure you want to go back there?" Caitlin said. "All this talk about danger and spirits and messages from dead people makes me nervous."

"I want to ask The Great Sybil some questions," Ellen said, "and I won't get to the fair again without my parents."

Caitlin nodded sympathetically. "Say no more," she said. "My mom would never let me visit The Great Sybil, either. Do you want me to tell Corey anything if he shows up? Should I ask him to stay here until you come back?"

"I doubt he'll be back. He and Nicholas planned to ride on every ride and eat something from every food booth. Corey's been saving his allowance for weeks so he could blow it all at the fair."

"Maybe the great danger is that he'll get sick from eating too much junk food at the fair," Caitlin said.

"Not when he's with Mrs. Warren. She's really careful about good nutrition. Whenever Nicholas comes to our house, he always wants candy because he never gets it at home; Nicholas says his mother would rather eat broccoli than fudge."

Spectators poured into the arena as the exhibitors led their sheep into position. Bleats and baas filled the air, along with broadcast directions from the judges, telling the exhibitors how to line up.

Ellen started down the steps, eager to see The Great Sybil again. Now that she was over the first shock and had thought about it awhile, the idea of being able to communicate with Grandpa excited her. If she really could get a message and prove that it was from him, maybe Grandma would stop crying so much. And maybe her own heart would heal. It wouldn't seem as bad to have Grandpa gone if she knew his spirit still existed.

Behind her, Caitlin said, "Wait. I'll go with you. I've seen Ben show his sheep before but I've never seen someone get a message from a spirit."

Ellen shook her head. "It's nice of you to offer," she said, "but I know you want to watch the sheep competition and it's almost ready to start."

"I don't want you going back there alone," Caitlin said firmly, as she followed Ellen to the exit. "This whole thing is too weird."

Ellen smiled gratefully at her friend. "I could wait and go after Ben shows his sheep," she said.

"No," Caitlin said. "This is more important than sheep."

They left the show arena and headed toward The Great Sybil's trailer.

◈ ◈ ◈

COREY DASHED after the man. When he caught him, he planned to grab the shopping bag and summon help. As soon as the police found the victim's wallet in the man's shopping bag, they would arrest the man. Probably the woman's purse was still in the shopping bag, too. Corey might get his picture in the paper yet.

The fairgrounds were crowded, making it difficult for the man to move fast without attracting attention. Since he didn't know anyone was chasing him, Corey gained on him quickly.

Just outside one of the exhibit halls, Corey caught up. He approached the man from behind and grabbed the shopping bag, pulling it out of the startled man's grasp. He tried to yell, "Help!" at the same time but he only managed a faint wheeze.

"Give me that!" the man said, as he tried to take back the bag.

Corey crossed his arms and held the bag handles tightly against his chest. He looked around him for one of the uniformed security guards who had responded when the woman's purse was stolen, but none was in sight.

"Why, you sneaky little thief!" the man said. He grabbed Corey's shoulder and turned to two teenaged boys who stood nearby. "This kid is trying to steal my bag," he said.

The boys instantly grabbed Corey's arm and pried his hands loose from the shopping bag. "That was a stupid move, kid," one of them said.

"*He's* the thief," Corey rasped but in addition to having no

44

voice, he was out of breath from running and he could tell the boys did not understand him.

The boys handed the bag back to the man.

"Thank you," he said.

Corey glared at him. This time he paid attention to the man's appearance. Medium height. Brown hair. Dark blue shirt and pants. A gold wristwatch. There was nothing remarkable about the man's appearance and Corey realized that he probably dressed in a nondescript way on purpose. If he wore a wild-colored plaid shirt or a T-shirt with a saying on the front, witnesses would be able to remember him. This way, he blended into the crowd and slipped away unnoticed.

"Are you going to call the cops?" one of the teenagers asked.

"No," the man said. "He has probably learned a lesson."

In frustration, Corey tried to wriggle free. He knew the man didn't want to call the cops because if the police came they would discover who the guilty person really was.

The man turned and walked toward the entrance of the building.

Corey twisted and jerked. He pointed at the man's shopping bag and tried to whisper, "Thief."

"Knock it off, kid," one of the teenagers said. He and his buddy, each firmly holding one of Corey's arms, ushered him away from the building. "You're lucky that guy didn't turn you in," the older boy continued. "If you keep this up, you'll be spending the night in the juvenile detention center."

The two boys kept a tight grip on Corey until they had walked for several minutes. Corey glared at them, studying their faces and memorizing what they wore. When the police finally arrested that pickpocket, Corey intended to give a complete description of these two boys. Maybe they would be arrested, too, for obstructing justice. Maybe *they* would spend the night in the juvenile detention center.

◈ ◈ ◈

AS ELLEN and Caitlin approached The Great Sybil's trailer, a white-haired woman was walking away from it. When she saw the two girls, she smiled and said, "Are you girls going to have your fortunes told?" Without waiting for them to answer, she went on, "It's well worth the price. The Great Sybil gave me the most wonderful news."

"She did?" Caitlin said.

The woman dabbed at her eyes but Ellen could tell her tears were happy ones. "Harold is at peace," the woman said. "I can stop worrying about him."

Wondering who Harold was, Ellen said, "How did The Great Sybil know?"

"Oh, she talks to the spirits," the woman said, "and they answer her. She specifically asked if Harold is all right and she was told, yes, he is. I can't tell you how much better I feel. I've been terribly worried about Harold. He wasn't ready to go, you know. He didn't want to leave me and he wanted to watch the grandchildren grow up. It happened so fast; we didn't have time to adjust to his sickness and, boom, he was gone. Ever since, all these months, I've worried that Harold couldn't rest in peace because . . ."

Ellen broke in to ask, "Did the spirits answer in writing?" She felt rude for interrupting but she had a feeling the woman would talk all day, given half a chance.

"Writing? How could spirits write anything?"

"They talked, then?" Caitlin said. "You heard someone?"

"Oh, no, my dear. I heard nothing. If I could hear such

things myself, I wouldn't need to pay a spiritualist, now would I? The Great Sybil heard the spirits and told me what they said."

"But how do you know she got an answer?" Caitlin said. "What if she made it up?"

The woman frowned. "Why would she do that? She never knew Harold. She can't possibly care if he is happy or not." The woman's smile returned. "I'm going to be able to sleep tonight, without taking a sleeping pill, for the first time since Harold passed on. The Great Sybil said I won't need pills anymore, now that I know Harold is at peace."

"I'm glad for you," Ellen said.

"Me, too," Caitlin said. She nudged Ellen and started to walk on. "It was nice talking to you," she said over her shoulder.

"When you girls get your fortunes told," the woman said, "I hope your news is as good as mine." She walked away, smiling and nodding at everyone she passed.

When the woman was no longer within hearing range, Caitlin said, "Do you think The Great Sybil really got a message about that woman's husband, or do you think she pretended, knowing what the woman wanted to hear?"

Ellen shrugged. "Does it matter? Either way, the woman is happy."

"I guess most people believe what they want to believe," Caitlin said.

"The trouble is," Ellen said, "I don't know what I want to believe. One part of me thinks it would be great if I could communicate with Grandpa. Another part of me says I'm asking for trouble if I try again. Also, there's Corey to consider, assuming he is 'the small one' in the message. If he is going to be in danger, I want to help him and I don't see how I can, without more information."

They had reached the ticket booth. "Hello," Ellen said to the man inside.

He barely glanced up from the newspaper he held before he said, "Sorry. You have to be eighteen or over."

"The Great Sybil told me I could come back without paying."

The man put down his paper and looked directly at her. "Aren't you the kid who was here earlier today?"

"Yes. I need to see her again."

"Sorry. She's out."

Ellen and Caitlin looked at each other. Their eyes agreed: *He's lying.*

Ellen, with Caitlin right behind her, marched to the door of the trailer and knocked.

"Hey!" the man called after them. "I told you Sybil isn't in."

The door opened.

"I am glad you returned," The Great Sybil said.

The man stepped out of the booth and hurried toward them. "Sybil," he said, "I don't think you should do this."

"I have to," The Great Sybil said. "Please come in, Ellen. And?"

"This is my friend Caitlin," Ellen said. "I told her about the automatic writing."

"Welcome, Caitlin. Pure one."

Caitlin looked questioningly at Ellen as they stepped inside.

"Caitlin," explained The Great Sybil, "is from the Greek name Katharos, meaning 'pure one.' It honors St. Catherine of Alexandria who escaped martyrdom on a spiked wheel in the fourth century."

"No kidding," said Caitlin.

"Be seated, please."

Ellen sat on the couch, leaving room for Caitlin to sit beside her. The Great Sybil sat on the same chair as before. "Do you wish to try again to contact the spirits?" The Great Sybil asked.

"Yes. I want to ask who the message is from and when the danger will be."

The Great Sybil nodded.

"You'll need the paper and pencil again," Caitlin reminded her.

Ellen reached in her shoulder bag and removed her notebook and pencil.

"Maybe you will get a spoken message this time," Caitlin said to The Great Sybil. "Maybe the spirits will speak to you."

"No," The Great Sybil said. "It is Ellen who will receive any messages." Ellen wondered why she sounded sad; she had seemed thrilled earlier, when the automatic writing occurred.

Ellen carried the pencil and notebook to the table and sat opposite The Great Sybil. She kept her hands on the table, with the pencil poised, ready to write. "I'm ready," she said.

The Great Sybil dimmed the lights and said the same calming words she had used before, about deep breaths and looking at the sky.

This time, although Ellen kept her eyes closed, she remained tense. Instead of imagining blue skies and fluffy clouds, Ellen's mind focused on the pencil she held. She gripped it tightly, expecting it to jolt into a frenzied scribbling.

"Ellen has a question, loving spirits," The Great Sybil said.

"She needs your help in knowing when the little one will face danger."

Nothing happened.

"We come to you in love," The Great Sybil said. "We ask you to tell us when to expect the danger."

They waited. The pencil remained still.

"Is the one who sent the message here with us? If you are, please let us know your identity."

Nothing. After five minutes of silence that seemed to Ellen more like an hour, they gave up.

"The spirits do not always choose to answer us," The Great Sybil said, after Ellen had opened her eyes and the lights were bright again. "Or perhaps they do not always hear our requests. We will have to try another time."

As Ellen and Caitlin walked away from The Great Sybil's trailer, Caitlin said, "If I were you, I would forget all about that so-called message. Before you went in there the first time, I was positive that she was a fake. Then you convinced me that the automatic writing really happened. Now I think it was all a hoax, after all. The reason it didn't work this time is that I was there, watching."

"When it happened, it seemed so real."

Caitlin unwrapped a stick of gum and offered half to Ellen. "Maybe so, but it is odd that you would get a message when you were there alone but nothing happened when I was looking. If the whole thing was genuine, why didn't it happen the second time? If there is really danger in Corey's future, and the spirits want to help, why did the spirits ignore you?"

"Maybe I was too nervous. I couldn't relax this time; I kept waiting for the pencil to start writing."

Caitlin said, "I think it was all a trick. Maybe she does it with magnets or some kind of ink that's already on the table but it's invisible until it touches paper or—oh, I don't know how but I think it was all faked somehow, just like she pretended the spirits spoke to her and told her what that woman wanted to hear about her husband."

"That was different," Ellen said. "That woman asked a specific question. And her message was not in writing."

"If a person is dishonest in one situation," Caitlin said, "how can you trust them anywhere?"

They entered the sheep arena just as the judges began handing ribbons to the owners of the champion sheep.

"Look!" said Caitlin. "Ben got a red ribbon; that's second place."

Ellen said, "I'm sorry I've ruined your day. You missed seeing Ben show his sheep and we've hardly gone to any of the exhibits yet, all because I wanted to get my fortune told."

"Don't worry about it," Caitlin said. "The Great Sybil was more interesting than any exhibit. Besides, Mom and I are coming tomorrow. I can see the rest of the exhibits then."

"In that case," Ellen said, "would you mind if we go home early? I'm worn out."

As the girls walked to the bus stop, Ellen was glad tomorrow was the last day of the fair. She wanted The Great Sybil and her tricks to leave town as soon as possible. *If* they were tricks.

Everything Caitlin said about the automatic writing being faked made sense but deep inside herself, Ellen still believed she had received a true message. It might be possible to make the writing appear on the paper but how could anyone have caused Ellen's hand to jerk without touching her? How could her inability to control her own body be a trick?

Corey was not home yet when Ellen arrived. She tried to

read but she couldn't concentrate; she flipped the TV from channel to channel and saw nothing interesting. What's the matter with me? she thought. Ever since Grandpa died she had felt edgy, as if she expected another tragedy. Now her uneasiness was multiplied tenfold as she listened for Corey to burst in, chattering about what he and Nicholas did at the fair.

I never thought I'd be eager to hear my brother's voice, she thought, trying to laugh away her tension. Usually when Corey was home, she wanted to plug her ears.

She was sure Corey was perfectly fine. After all, Mrs. Warren was with him and she was one of those fussy mother-hen women who hardly let Nicholas out of her sight. Nothing could happen to Corey when he was with Mrs. Warren. Still, Ellen would be glad when Corey was safely home.

CHAPTER
◈ 7 ◈

"SOME KID knows what we're doing."

Mitch Lagrange opened the trunk of his car and put the MADE IN THE U.S.A. shopping bag inside, next to the five other MADE IN THE U.S.A. bags that were already there.

"How could he?" Joan asked. "We haven't worked the same area twice all day and no one has acted the least bit suspicious. How could some kid catch on?"

"I don't know, but I'm telling you this boy has it figured out. He ran after me, grabbed my bag, and tried to accuse me." Mitch slammed the trunk shut. "Luckily, there's something wrong with his voice and he couldn't make himself heard. I pretended he was trying to take the bag away from me and two teenagers stepped in and acted like big macho heroes. They held the kid while I walked away from him."

Mitch unlocked the car door and slid behind the wheel. Joan got in the passenger's side and Alan sat in back.

"How old was he?" Joan asked.

Mitch shrugged. "About the same age as Alan, I'd guess. Maybe eight or nine."

"What does he look like?"

"Just an average-looking kid, except he had a big Batman bandage on his face. Brown hair. Jeans. A T-shirt with elephants on it—from a zoo, I think."

"Did his parents see you?" she asked.

"He was alone."

"Are you sure? If he was only eight or nine, somebody must have brought him to the fair."

"There wasn't anybody with him when he ran after me," Mitch said, "but by now he's probably blabbed to his parents or whoever brought him. We'll have to quit. We can sit here and wait until Tucker gets his dinner break."

"No!" said Alan. "You promised we could work until Uncle Tucker can meet us."

"I didn't know some junior detective would show up and accuse me of stealing."

"I want some more ice cream."

"You've had enough ice cream," Mitch said. "We've bought a dozen ice-cream cones today."

"I never get to finish them. I always have to pretend I'm falling and spill them on the ground."

Joan chuckled. "You're getting to be a fine little actor," she said. "I almost believed you myself last time, the way you cried and carried on."

Alan smiled. "Let's move to Hollywood," he said. "Maybe I'll get a job in a TV show."

"I don't like it," Mitch said. "Maybe we shouldn't even wait to eat dinner with Tucker. All we need is some little kid going to the cops."

"Today has been the best day of the whole summer," Alan said. "Maybe even the best day of my whole life. We got tons of wallets and purses. We even got that video camera. Let's keep that. Can we, Mitch?"

"Be quiet, Alan. I'm trying to think."

"This is way more fun than delivering a dumb old car," Alan said. "And you said we could do it all afternoon. You promised."

"Alan!"

Alan said, "Mom! You promised, too. You said if I did my part good, I could have some of the money. You said we could do it until Uncle Tucker's dinner break."

"We did say that, Mitch," Joan said. "Now that we know about the boy, we can watch for him. There can't be more than one kid that age running around with a Batman bandage on his face and elephants on his shirt. If we spot him, we'll back off."

"I don't like it," Mitch repeated. "We've done well this year; we've made a lot of money. I don't want to blow it over a two-bit pickpocket incident."

"Just work until dinnertime, when we meet Tucker," Joan said. "We promised Alan and it's been such fun, working a crowd again. It's like when I was first on my own and had to pick pockets in order to eat."

"If we get caught by the cops, your meals will be provided by the state—in jail."

"First offenders get off with a warning."

"Not always." Mitch knew Joan did not fully understand

55

what a risk she was asking him to take. How could she, when Mitch had never told her about his past? She did not realize the depth of his fear. She did not know how important it was for Mitch never to be picked up by the police.

"Let's tell Tucker about the kid," Joan suggested, "and Tucker can watch for him, too, just like he watches for the guards now. If the kid shows up, Tucker signals us, and we beat it out of there."

Mitch looked dubious. "That platform of Tucker's is a long way up and there are an awful lot of little kids at the fair."

"Not wearing big Batman bandages on their cheeks."

"Please, Mitch?" Alan said. "I want to do my ice-cream trick some more. This is the most fun I've had in my whole life. Please?"

"No," Mitch said. "No more. We're going to sit right here and wait for Tucker."

"Nobody ever keeps their promises," Alan said. He put his head down on the seat and started to cry.

"You can sit here, if you want," Joan said. "Alan and I are going back to the fair. We'll work alone."

Alan's tears instantly vanished.

Joan and Alan got out of the car.

"Don't do this," Mitch said.

"I worked by myself for years, before I met you."

Mitch looked at Joan and Alan, side by side, glaring at him. It was that way too often—Joan and Alan on one side, Mitch alone on the other. He wondered if the three of them would ever seem like a real family.

"All right," Mitch said. "We'll tell Tucker. We can use the same signal we have for fair guards or cops." He got slowly out of the car.

"Lock the doors," Joan said. "You don't know what sort of people go through this parking lot."

Alan laughed.

The three headed back through the main entrance of the fairgrounds, showing the ink stamps on the backs of their hands that allowed them to get in without paying an entrance fee. Their first stop was the commercial exhibit building, where Mitch picked up another free shopping bag. Next they headed for The River of Fear to tell Mitch's brother, Tucker, to watch for a boy with a Batman bandage.

"I want another chocolate marshmallow ice-cream cone," Alan said. "I hardly got to eat any of the last one."

◇ ◇ ◇

AS SOON as the teenagers let go of his arms, Corey headed for the sheep arena. There was no use trying to catch the thief when he had no voice. Corey would find Ellen and she would give him something to write on and he would write down his description of the thief and Ellen would go with him to look for the man. Ellen could be a hero, too, though Corey would still be the main hero because he was the one who saw the man stealing.

When Corey arrived at the sheep arena, three people were walking their sheep in a slow circle. One held a large purple rosette, one held a blue ribbon, and one held a red ribbon. Corey recognized Caitlin's cousin; he was the one with the red ribbon.

Corey stood by the railing and watched the winning sheep parade around the arena for awhile before he began to climb the steps toward where Ellen and Caitlin had sat earlier. Partway up, he realized that Ellen and Caitlin were not there.

Corey looked all around the arena, thinking they had changed their seats, moved lower where they could see the sheep better.

They were gone. He must have just missed them, since he was certain they would have watched Ben show his sheep. Probably they had gone outside to get something to eat. He left the arena to look for Ellen.

Corey walked along a row of food booths, sniffing all the wonderful odors. Cotton candy. Hot dogs. Teriyaki stir-fry. Even though he was too full to eat anything more, it all smelled delicious.

He pressed his nose against the window of the funnel-cake booth. The cook squirted ribbons of batter in a circular motion into a vat of hot oil, going around and around in ever-larger circles, shaping each funnel cake like a miniature braided rug. The oil bubbled around them and the cakes quickly puffed up and turned golden brown. After each funnel cake was fried, the cook lifted it from the oil with a large slotted spoon, shaking the spoon to drain off the excess oil. He put the funnel cake on a paper plate, and sprinkled powdered sugar on it. Maybe, Corey thought, he could squeeze one funnel cake into his over-stuffed stomach.

Corey dug into his pocket and counted his money, dismayed to see how little he had left. How could it be gone so soon? He didn't even have enough to ride on The River of Fear. However, there was exactly enough to buy a funnel cake, and Corey did so, pointing at the cakes and holding up one finger so the cook knew what he wanted.

Tonight, he would ask his parents if they had some chores he could do to earn extra money. Maybe he could wash windows or mow the grass or weed the flower beds. If he could earn some money tonight, he and Nicholas could come back to the fair and ride The River of Fear together. Nicholas was sure to feel better by tomorrow and Corey's voice should be back by then, too. It would be great to ride and scream together.

He took a huge bite of funnel cake, sending a shower of powdered sugar down the front of his shirt. Yum. Chewing happily and making his plans for tomorrow, Corey strolled around the fairgrounds, looking for Ellen. She and Caitlin were not in the sheep barn; they were not on the merry-go-round; they were not in the Arts and Crafts exhibit, where Ellen always liked to go because she said it inspired her to make new things.

Some lumberjacks were putting on a show; Corey applauded as two men in spiked shoes raced to the top of a pole. He watched a man carve totem poles with a chain saw. The saw buzzed and whined as the man fashioned a bear from a cedar log.

When a loudspeaker announced that it was time for the pig races, Corey hurried with the crowd to a fenced area where five piglets waited to dash toward their food.

After the pig races, Corey returned to the sheep barn, intending to ask Ben if he knew where the girls were. Ben, however, was nowhere to be seen.

Corey decided he should call his parents, tell them what had happened, and ask them to come and get him. He hoped he would be able, with his hoarse voice, to make them hear enough to know what he was saying. If he couldn't, they might think it was a prank call and hang up.

He saw a public telephone at the front of one of the exhibit halls. He went there, picked up the receiver, and realized he needed a quarter before he could get a dial tone. He had no quarter. He had no money at all. Phooey. He probably shouldn't have bought that last funnel cake.

Well, he would just walk around and look for Ellen awhile longer. That would be more fun than going home, anyhow, and if he never found her, he could always go to a guard or the information booth and ask them to call his parents.

Corey wandered toward the merry-go-round. He liked the merry-go-round music and wished he had enough money to ride on one of the horses while he waited. He would choose the white horse with the blue and silver saddle.

"Win a genuine stuffed dinosaur! Only seventy-five cents!" When the merry-go-round stopped, Corey heard the man's voice and got angry all over again. If that man wasn't a crook, Corey would not have wasted so much of his money trying to win a dinosaur.

He decided to spy on the bottle booth. Maybe he could discover how the man cheated his customers. He would tell the police and they would come and arrest the man and the mayor would give Corey an award and all the other kids who tried to win a dinosaur and got cheated out of their money would come to the award ceremony and cheer and Corey would get his picture in the newspaper.

Corey sneaked along the narrow alleyway behind the food booths, darting quickly between buildings. When he was near the bottle booth, he crouched behind a large trash bin and peered out.

He wished he could disguise himself, so the bottle-booth man wouldn't recognize him. All the good spies he had read about wore disguises. He looked quickly around; no one could see him behind the trash bin. It was the perfect place to put on a costume, if only he had one.

Since he didn't, he would have to change his appearance as best he could. Corey picked at one corner of the Batman bandage, held it tightly and clenched his teeth. Taking a bandage off was worse than getting hurt in the first place. Silently he counted, *one, two, three*. On *three*, he yanked the Batman bandage from his face, wadded it up, and stuffed it in his pocket. Next he took off his T-shirt, turned it inside out so the zoo logo and the picture of the elephants didn't show, and put it back on. Using both hands, he mussed up his hair. He couldn't think of anything else he could do to change his appearance, so he peeked out and spied on the bottle booth.

As he watched, he heard The River of Fear spiel again. He wondered how it would feel to take the death-defying plunge down Whiplash Waterfall, to enter the Tunnel of Terror, and to meet the monsters of Mutilation Mountain. He would *have* to earn some money and return to the fair.

People kept walking between the trash bin and the bottle booth, making it difficult for Corey to see. He shifted and peeked out the other direction.

The woman and the boy who kept dropping his ice cream sauntered toward him. The child was licking another ice-cream cone.

Some people never learn, thought Corey, and just as he thought it, the boy tripped and fell, sending the ice-cream cone splattering into the dirt at the feet of a couple who were holding hands. The boy instantly began to cry. Corey watched as the couple tried to help the boy up but he only wailed louder.

Corey's mouth fell open in surprise. There was the man with the shopping bag! The thief! Corey stared as the man lifted a wallet out of the tote bag of the woman who was trying to help the boy. The man dropped the wallet into his MADE IN

THE U.S.A. shopping bag, exactly as he had dropped in the other woman's purse, earlier. The couple, their attention focused on the crying child, never noticed him. Neither did any of the people nearby. The kid was having a first-class tantrum over his ice-cream cone.

Corey leaped from behind the trash container. Waving both arms wildly and forcing unintelligible squeaks from his raw throat, he rushed toward the man with the bag.

CHAPTER

◈ 8 ◈

THE BOY stopped crying, pointed at Corey, and yelled, "Mom! Look!"

The helpful couple, who still did not realize they were the victims of a thief, looked at Corey in surprise.

The man with the shopping bag took one look at Corey and said, "That's him," before he whirled around, and ran. He wove in and out between people, elbowing them out of his way and not caring who he bumped into.

Corey rushed after him.

The boy said loudly, "Let's go home, Mom. I didn't want that dumb ice-cream cone, anyway."

The victimized couple looked at each other, shrugged, and walked away.

As Corey dashed past the woman and the boy who kept dropping his ice-cream cones, the woman put her hand on Corey's shoulder, stopping him.

"Is something wrong, little boy?" she asked. "Do you need help?"

Corey pointed toward the man and tried to say, "Thief."

"I'm sorry," the woman said. "I can't understand you. You'll have to speak up."

Corey tried to leave but the woman clung to his shoulder, holding him back. By the time he could push her hand off and dart away from her, the momentary distraction had caused him to lose sight of the man.

Where had he gone? Corey kept moving as he looked frantically for the thief. The man could not disappear into thin air.

◈   ◈   ◈

MITCH'S HEART thudded in his chest. He should never have let Joan talk him into this. He looked around for a trash can, planning to throw in the shopping bag, contents and all. If the kid caught up with him, there would be no evidence.

Instead, he saw a fair security guard sauntering toward him. Mitch's mouth went dry. That fool, Tucker! Not only did he miss the kid, he missed a guard, as well. He glanced upward at the platform where his brother was supposed to be keeping watch, wondering how his own flesh and blood could be so stupid.

The guard kept coming. Mitch couldn't turn back, not with that crazy kid after him. He didn't want to pass the guard, either. Impulsively, he ran toward The River of Fear platform. He would give the bag to Tucker and let him dispose of the wallet.

A flash of white above him made Corey look up. It was the shopping bag. The thief was halfway up the steps to The River of Fear.

Corey charged after him. There was nothing at the top of these steps except The River of Fear platform. The thief would be trapped up there and the man who runs the ride could call for help. Corey climbed as fast as he could, keeping to the right because people who had just been on The River of Fear were coming down. He wished he could still speak, to tell them he was chasing a thief. If they knew, they would want to stay and watch.

As he climbed, he heard the spiel and the roar of Whiplash Waterfall and the terrified screams of the people who were still riding. Too bad Nicholas wasn't with him.

On the platform above Corey, Mitch spoke rapidly to Tucker. "The kid's after me; why didn't you signal?"

"I never saw him," Tucker said.

"I have to get out of here," Mitch said.

"Get on the ride. No one can see you in there."

"How long does it last?"

"Five minutes."

"Just long enough for the kid to get a guard and be waiting when I get off," Mitch said. He glanced nervously over his shoulder.

"You could go down the back stairs," Tucker said, "the ones I use for maintenance."

"Good. Where are they?"

"You can't get to the back stairs until the ride stops."

"I can't wait!" Mitch stormed over to the edge of the platform, looked down, and stormed back. "The kid's coming up."

"Why did you come up here?" Tucker asked. "Why didn't you run into one of the buildings?"

"I didn't think he would see me come up here, but he did. I swear the kid has X-ray eyes."

"Let's put the kid on the ride."

Mitch's face relaxed into smile. "You're a genius, Tucker. It must run in the family. And once he's on it, in the middle somewhere, where he can't be seen or heard, you can stop the ride. Keep him inside for awhile until Joan and I get away from here."

"No problem," Tucker said. "This ride breaks down all the time; no one will think anything of it if I say it needs repair again."

"Get the other people off first. We don't want anyone helping him."

Corey clambered onto the platform. The thief stood on the far side. Corey went straight to the ride operator, mouthing the word, "Help!"

"What's wrong, sonny?" the man said. "Calm down now and tell old Tucker your problem."

To the right, a string of boats emerged from the main, enclosed part of the ride and stopped beside the platform. A group of shrieking, laughing people got off and started down the steps.

"Help," Corey repeated.

"Wait a minute," Tucker said. "I can't hear you."

Corey gripped Tucker's arm until the people were gone. Then he pointed at the man with the shopping bag and tried to say, "Thief." He wondered why the thief just stood there, with his back to Corey, looking down at the fairgrounds. Didn't he realize that Corey had followed him up the steps?

"Come over here, sonny," Tucker said, "where I can hear you better." He stepped closer to where people board the ride.

Corey followed. "Thief," Corey rasped again, as he pointed at the man.

The last customer went down the steps. The thief still looked away from Corey.

Tucker bent so that his face was level with Corey's. "Now then, sonny," he said, "what is it you want to tell me?"

Corey tried again to say, "Thief."

"Thief?" Tucker said. "Is that what you are saying? Thief?"

Corey nodded and pointed at the man's shopping bag.

"He steals things and hides them in the bag?" Tucker said.

Corey's head bobbed up and down vigorously. Someone finally understood him.

"You are a brave boy to chase a thief by yourself," Tucker said.

Corey grinned, glad that someone appreciated his courage.

"Get on with it!" The thief strode toward them across the platform.

Corey stayed close to Tucker.

"This boy claims you've been stealing, Mitch," Tucker said. "It isn't nice to steal things. Didn't your mother teach you anything?"

The two men grinned at each other.

How did he know the thief's name? Corey wondered. Why was the thief smiling? An uneasy feeling spread through Corey's insides. It was odd that the thief had just stood there while Corey talked to Tucker and odd that Tucker called the man by name and odd that both of them were smiling. Too odd.

He should not have followed the thief up here; he should have let that boy's mother help him or he should have found a guard. Corey took a step away from Tucker but Mitch quickly blocked his way.

Tucker turned some knobs on the control panel. The volume on the spiel boomed louder.

The stairs were the only escape route but Mitch stood between Corey and the stairs. Corey looked around him, forced a wide smile onto his face, and waved, pretending that someone had just joined them on the platform.

When Mitch turned to see who Corey was waving at, Corey made a dash for the steps.

As Corey darted past Mitch toward the top of the steps, two strong hands clamped down on his shoulders.

"Hey!" Corey squeaked.

Mitch spun Corey around, lifted him like a rag doll, and dropped him into one of the boats. Even if Corey had been able to make a sound, it happened too fast for him to say anything.

Corey landed with a *thunk* in the bottom of the boat. As he sat up, he saw the thief put his arm on Tucker's shoulder.

"Nice try, kid," Tucker said, "but you can't trick Mitch Lagrange that easily."

They laughed while Tucker pulled a large lever.

The River of Fear ride started. The boat Corey was in sped forward past the left end of the platform and into the enclosed part of the ride. Corey knelt at the bottom of the boat, clutching the sides.

Seconds later, he began his death-defying descent down Whiplash Waterfall.

CHAPTER

• 9 •

"GRANDPA?" Ellen whispered. "Are you here?"

Tick. Tick. Tick. Ellen had never noticed before that the clock on her bedside table made such a loud noise. She tried to ignore it, concentrating on the pencil and paper in her hands.

"If you can hear me, Grandpa, I need your help. I got a message today and I have to know if it is from you. If it is, could you please send me some sort of sign?"

Tick. Tick. Tick.

Ellen waited, hardly breathing. Surely, if Grandpa could hear her, he would grant her request. He would let her know, somehow, that he was there.

"I love you, Grandpa, and I miss you. We all do. It would help us a lot if you could send me a sign, to let me know you hear me."

The pencil was still.

Ellen sighed, opened her eyes, and looked at the clock. Six-fifteen. She had been trying for nearly half an hour without success. She pushed her chair away from her desk and stood up. Prince, Ellen's dog, woke up, stretched, and came over and sat beside Ellen. He lifted one paw, the way he did when Ellen told him to shake hands.

Absentmindedly, Ellen reached down to shake Prince's paw but as her hand closed around his foot, she stopped. Grandpa had taught Prince that trick. When the rest of the family had despaired of ever teaching Prince anything more than "sit" and "stay," Grandpa had worked with him day after day until Prince finally caught on. Whenever Grandpa came to visit, Prince always ran to him and shook hands.

Was that the sign? Had Grandpa told Prince to shake just now, or had Prince merely held up his paw to get Ellen's attention?

Feeling unsteady, Ellen put one hand on her dresser for support. She immediately pulled back when she realized her hand had inadvertently landed on the silver elephant that Grandpa gave her for Christmas last year.

"His trunk is up," he had told her, "which means he's holding good luck. Good luck for you."

Ellen thought she had never seen anything so exquisite. The lines in the elephant's hide, the tiny tail, the eyes—everything was perfect. She had worn it daily, until the accident. She had not worn it since. Why was her hand drawn to it now?

"Ellen! Dinner's ready." Ellen jumped at the sound of her mother's voice.

My nerves are shot, she realized, as she headed toward the kitchen, with Prince at her heels.

"I certainly didn't think Mrs. Warren would keep Corey and Nicholas at the fair this late," Mrs. Streater said, as she dished up salad. "They've been gone since nine this morning."

70

"You know how boys are," Mr. Streater said. "They probably begged to go on every ride."

"When I saw them, they looked like they were having a great time," Ellen said. "They didn't even stay to watch the sheep show."

"Do you know what Corey told me last night?" Mr. Streater said. "He said the reason he wanted to go on the rides was so he could scream a lot."

"I warned him about that, with his bad throat," Mrs. Streater said, "but I don't think he was listening. He was going on about some gruesome ride he plans to invent."

Ellen rolled her eyes while Mr. Streater chuckled.

"I thought they would be home in time for dinner," Mrs. Streater said.

"Corey will not be hungry after a day at the fair," said Mr. Streater. "Remember how much he ate last time?"

"When I saw him," Ellen said, "he had a big plate of curly fries."

"Julia Warren doesn't usually let Nicholas eat a lot of fatty food," Mrs. Streater said. "I hope she didn't let those boys go off on their own."

"You worry too much," said Mr. Streater. "Enjoy the quiet while you can; Corey will be home soon enough and then we'll have to hear every detail of his day at the fair. Twice."

"Mrs. Warren was with them in the sheep arena," Ellen said.

"Good."

Although Ellen tried to reassure her mother, it increased her own nervousness to listen to her mother's worries. The later it got with no sign of Corey, the more Ellen wondered if she should tell her parents about the message.

What if Corey wasn't home yet because he was in terrible trouble?

"Have some lasagna, Ellen," Mrs. Streater said. "It's Father's veggie recipe."

Ellen took the pan her mother handed her. Veggie lasagna. Grandpa's favorite meal—the only recipe that he personally ever prepared.

Ellen chewed the noodles, tomato sauce, cheese, and spinach. Was *this* a sign from Grandpa? Mom had not made veggie lasagna in months. Why did she choose tonight?

"I was in the mood to cook this morning," Mrs. Streater said, "so I made a double recipe and froze some."

This morning. It can't be a sign from Grandpa, Ellen thought. The lasagna was made this morning, before I got the message, before I asked for a sign. I'm getting crazy, thinking about this.

She tried to eat but nothing tasted good. "May I be excused?" she said and, when her mother nodded, she left the table and went back to her bedroom. She wandered aimlessly around for awhile, looked out the window, and finally picked up a magazine. She glanced at the cover and realized it was the magazine that Grandpa had bought a subscription to, as a treat when Ellen got all *A*s on her report card. She put it down, refusing to let herself think that the magazine was a sign telling her that Grandpa was here.

She took the message out of her pocket and read it again. *It is for you to know that the smaller one faces great danger. He will pay for his mistake. It is for you to know that the paths of destiny can be changed and the smaller one will need your help to change his. You will know when it is time. Do not ignore this warning.*

Maybe, instead of trying to contact Grandpa, she should try to contact any of the spirits, just as The Great Sybil had the first time. Maybe the message was from Ellen's guardian angel. Or maybe it was from some other spirit.

Once again, Ellen picked up a piece of paper and pen. She sat at her desk, with the window shade down and the lights off. She closed her eyes, breathed deeply several times, and whispered, "Loving spirits, do you have a message for me? I come to you in love and friendship, asking for help to protect my brother."

She waited a few moments and then spoke again. "If Corey will need my help, spirits, please send another message and tell me when."

The pen jerked into action, rubbing the paper violently. It lasted barely two seconds. By the time Ellen could react, it was over.

She opened her eyes. The paper held a single word, printed in large capital letters that slanted to the left: URGENT.

The first message had said, "You will know when it is time." The second message seemed to say, the time is now.

The back of Ellen's neck prickled. It was no longer important to her who the messages might be from. What mattered was that Corey needed help, and he needed it now.

Trying to act calm, Ellen returned to her parents and said, "Something strange happened and I want to tell you about it."

Mr. and Mrs. Streater, alerted by the tone of Ellen's voice that this was no ordinary discussion, stopped what they were doing and paid close attention.

Ellen started at the beginning, and told every detail of her time with The Great Sybil. When she got to the part where

The Great Sybil asked if she had recently lost a loved one, Mrs. Streater said, "Oh, Ellen."

Mr. Streater said, "What hogwash! I'm surprised you would take such nonsense seriously."

"I thought the message might be from Grandpa," Ellen said, "so when I got home, I tried talking to him. I asked him to let me know if he was sending a message. I thought, if Grandpa's spirit is here, he could give me some sign."

Mr. Streater stood up and began pacing back and forth while Ellen continued.

"As soon as I asked for a sign," Ellen said, "Prince came over and put up his paw to shake hands. Grandpa taught him that trick. I didn't say, 'shake,' or give Prince any signal; he just did it on his own."

"Now, Ellen . . ." Mr. Streater began but Ellen continued to talk.

"Then I came downstairs and we had veggie lasagna for dinner, Grandpa's recipe. And when I looked around for something to read, I picked up the *Earth Watch* magazine that Grandpa gave me a subscription to and it seems like those could all be signs that Grandpa sent the messages." She didn't mention the elephant. It was the last gift Grandpa gave her and perhaps the most important sign of all but she didn't want to talk about it.

"Those were not signs from Grandpa," Mr. Streater said firmly. "They are only proof that a person lives on in the memory of his loved ones because of what that person did when he was alive. Grandpa will always be a part of your life and you'll think of him every time Prince shakes hands or you eat veggie lasagna or read your magazine or go to the zoo or do any number of other things that you and Grandpa did

74

together." He put his hands on Ellen's shoulders and looked directly into her eyes. "They are memories," he said, "Not supernatural signs."

"But what about the messages?" Ellen said. "The first one might have been some trick that The Great Sybil did but the second one came when I was alone in my room."

"What second one?" Mr. Streater said.

"After dinner, I tried to contact the spirits, the way The Great Sybil did. I was worried about Corey and I asked the spirits to let me know if Corey needs help."

"And?" Mr. Streater said.

"And it happened again. The pencil moved by itself. It wrote, URGENT."

She held out the piece of paper and Mr. Streater looked at it. As he slowly sat down, he said, "I don't know what is going on here, but I don't like it one bit."

The telephone rang and Mrs. Streater answered.

"Hello?" she said. "He isn't here. Is this Nicholas? Where are you? Isn't Corey with you? Let me speak to your mother, please."

As Ellen listened to her mother's side of the conversation, her stomach began to turn flip-flops.

After she hung up, Mrs. Streater said, "Nicholas got sick and Julia brought him home. Corey stayed at the fair."

"What?" Mr. Streater jumped to his feet. "She left Corey there by himself?"

Mrs. Streater's voice, when she answered, sounded brittle, as if it would shatter into tiny pieces at any moment. "She thought Corey was with Ellen. She left him where they were showing the sheep and she said she knew you saw him, Ellen, and Corey promised to stay with you."

"I *did* see him," Ellen said. "But I saw Mrs. Warren and Nicholas, too. I didn't know they were going to leave without Corey."

"No one is blaming you. It was a misunderstanding."

"How long ago did they leave him?" Mr. Streater asked.

Mrs. Streater leaned against the table, as if she was afraid she would fall over without support. "Julia said she and Nicholas have been home since three-thirty."

Minutes later, Mr. and Mrs. Streater and Ellen were in their car, driving toward the fairgrounds.

Silently, Ellen urged her father to drive faster. *Hurry*, Ellen thought. *Please hurry! Corey is in terrible danger.*

CHAPTER

◈ 10 ◈

COREY GRIPPED the side of the boat, certain he was going to be flung out as the boat sped down the waterfall.

The boat had a seat, with a safety belt, and a metal bar that pulled down across the lap of someone who was seated properly. But the men had shoved Corey into the boat and started the ride before Corey could use the safety devices. He stayed on the floor, clung to the side of the boat, and tried to keep his balance as the boat rushed forward.

After the boat plunged over the crest of the waterfall, it twisted around curves, jerked upward, and then dropped straight down, as if a trapdoor had opened underneath it. Corey's knees left the floor and slammed back down. Corey had thought the roller coaster was exciting; this made the roller coaster seem like one of the kiddieland rides.

The boat zoomed around a curve and then slowed as it entered the blackness of the Tunnel of Terror. Corey blinked, trying to adjust his eyes to the dark. A huge hairy hand, holding a dagger, appeared just ahead. As the boat approached, the dagger, dripping blood, plunged toward Corey. Corey ducked, his heart drumming rapidly.

A cold wind blasted him from the right; when he looked, he saw a scarred, one-eyed face and heard a horrible laugh.

It's all fake, Corey told himself. It's just sound effects and tricks, like in the Historical Society's haunted house that he and Ellen helped in last Halloween.

A large wolf-like animal rushed toward him, foaming at the mouth. Just inches from Corey's boat, the wolf ducked down and then, as the boat passed, it leaped up again, snapping its huge jaws at Corey.

Corey leaned away from it, only to feel something slimy on the back of his neck. He gasped and twisted around. Wet seaweed dangled from above.

A sea serpent slithered partway out of the water; its claws reached toward Corey, trying to grab him and pull him into the water. The boat began to rock, throwing Corey violently from side to side.

Tears spilled down Corey's cheeks. Even if the sea serpent *was* fake, it was the creepiest thing he had ever seen. And maybe it was real. He no longer knew what to think or believe. He had thought the man who ran The River of Fear ride would help him and instead he was a crook, too, and maybe they were never going to stop the ride and let Corey get off. What if that was how they planned to keep Corey from talking to a guard? Maybe Corey was going to keep going around and around on the ride, diving down Whiplash Waterfall and through the Tunnel of Terror for the rest of the night.

And, he knew, there was more ahead. He knew, from listening to The River of Fear spiel, that if he made it out of the Tunnel of Terror alive, he still had to face the monsters of Mutilation Mountain.

The sea serpent's claws came closer. More wet, slimy seaweed dropped from the ceiling and brushed against Corey's face. No matter which way he turned his head, fingers of seaweed reached for him. Corey smelled a dank, moldy odor. He screamed his silent scream, knowing he wasn't making any sound, feeling the hurt in his throat, but unable to stop himself.

The boat bounced upward, as if the monster were underneath it. The serpent's face emerged ahead of the boat now, its evil eyes gleaming red, and Corey was positive the boat and the serpent were going to collide. The serpent opened its huge jaws, revealing sharp fangs. The boat moved closer.

When the boat was inches from the serpent's open mouth, the boat stopped.

The dim light went out; the serpent's eyes ceased to glow. Corey was surrounded by total blackness.

All sound effects ended when the boat quit moving. Corey trembled in the bottom of the boat, waiting to see what would happen next.

Silence.

Blackness.

For a few moments, he thought this was just part of the ride and that, after a moment of stillness, something loud and ferocious and terrible would jump out at him. He gritted his teeth and braced himself but when the minutes stretched on and nothing happened, Corey realized that the ride had stopped.

Had the man stopped it on purpose or was it broken again? Whatever the reason, it was no longer running.

Corey was stuck in the middle of the Tunnel of Terror.

◈ ◈ ◈

"NO," the woman in the fair office said, as she looked at the picture of Corey that Mrs. Streater had in her wallet. "He has not come to the office for help. I've been here since noon. Are you sure he didn't go home with a friend?"

"Positive," Mr. Streater said.

"Did you have a meeting place selected, in case you became separated?"

"We didn't bring him," Mrs. Streater said. "He came with someone else."

"The merry-go-round," Ellen said. "Last year, when we came to the fair, we agreed to meet at the merry-go-round, if we got separated. Maybe Corey is waiting for us there."

"I suggest you look there," the woman said. "Meanwhile, I'll alert the security guards to watch for him. What is he wearing?"

Mrs. Streater started to describe Corey's clothing. Ellen added, "He has a big Batman bandage on his cheek."

"I'll have the guards look for him," the woman said.

Mr. and Mrs. Streater and Ellen hurried to the merry-go-round. Corey was not there.

"Let's check all of the most likely places, before we panic," Mr. Streater said. "You know how Corey is. If he's having fun, he probably hasn't even realized what time it is. No doubt he is wandering around, making up some fantastic tale about carousel horses that fly or pretending he's won first place in every competition and will have his picture in the newspaper.

Ellen, you look in the sheep barn. Maybe Corey is hanging around there, watching Caitlin's cousin."

"I'll check out the rows of food stands," Mrs. Streater said. "He always wants to eat everything they sell."

"I'll do the midway rides," Mr. Streater said. "Meet back here as soon as you can."

Corey was not in the sheep barn. Ellen's panic increased. If I ever needed help from a guardian angel, Ellen thought, now is the time. And any spirits who cared to guide her to Corey would be welcome, too.

Ellen rushed out of the sheep barn and ran toward The Great Sybil's trailer. The small ticket booth was empty. A sign on The Great Sybil's door said, CLOSED FOR DINNER. BACK IN 10 MINUTES.

Ellen knocked on the door. When there was no response, she pounded as hard as she could. "Sybil!" she called. "It's Ellen Streater. I need your help."

The door opened an inch. The Great Sybil peeked out.

"My brother didn't come home," Ellen said. "We think he's lost at the fair, or else something has happened to him."

The Great Sybil opened the door and motioned for Ellen to enter. She sat on one of the chairs and Ellen sat on the other.

"I tried the automatic writing at home, by myself," Ellen said. "I got another message. It said: URGENT."

"Oh, my," said The Great Sybil. "The smaller one needs your help right now."

"The trouble is, I don't know how to help him. I don't know where he is or what has happened."

"Let us begin," said The Great Sybil, as she dimmed the lights.

"I don't have anything to write with."

The Great Sybil opened a drawer on her side of the table and removed a yellow legal tablet and a pencil.

Ellen held them in front of her and forced herself to breathe deeply, trying to calm her jangling nerves.

"We beg for your help, loving spirits," said The Great Sybil, without any preliminaries. "Ellen needs guidance. Please enlighten her. Let her know where her brother is."

Silently, Ellen added her own plea. *I know Corey is in danger. Please help me, spirits. Please help me find him before it's too late.*

Tears formed behind Ellen's closed eyelids and she squeezed her eyes tightly shut.

"We await your message," said The Great Sybil.

"Please hurry," whispered Ellen. It was hard for her to keep her mind focused on the spirits. Her thoughts kept darting back to Corey and the various possibilities of where he might be. Should she be out searching for him instead of sitting here, hoping for a message that might never come?

"We await your message," The Great Sybil said softly.

Ellen wondered how the woman could be so calm. Why didn't she simply yell, "Hey, spirits! We need help fast!" If the angels or spirits or whomever she was talking to were as wise and loving as The Great Sybil said, they would understand the need to hurry.

"Please enlighten us," The Great Sybil droned.

Ellen opened her eyes. She couldn't waste any more time. "Sybil," she said.

The Great Sybil's eyes remained closed. Her hands were clasped tightly together as she silently beseeched the spirits for help.

As Ellen stared at the fortune-teller, the pencil leaped into motion. It jerked quickly across the paper, writing frantically, as if her hand were the mechanical hand of a robot and, once programmed, there was no way to stop it.

This time, of course, Ellen didn't try to stop it. If the message would help her find Corey, it didn't matter how she got it. The spirits could make her stand on her head and write with her toes, for all she cared, as long as Corey was safe.

The writing stopped. The pencil dropped from Ellen's hand. As soon as The Great Sybil turned the lights up, Ellen read the message aloud.

It was the same back-slanted handwriting as before. This time it said, *It is for you to know that there is darkness in the tunnel. The little one sees not. The sign is untrue. Go inside the darkness.*

"The little one sees not!" Ellen said. "That sounds like Corey is blind." The tears that she had been trying to hold back now trickled down her cheeks. "Why can't the spirits talk in plain language?" she asked. "This sounds like they know where Corey is, so why can't they just come out and tell us, instead of making it into a riddle?"

"You must remember," The Great Sybil said, "that the spirits are no longer of this world. It may be extremely difficult for them to send any message at all in a language that we can understand."

"It says the sign is untrue," Ellen said.

"That puzzles me. What sign? Perhaps it means the other messages." The Great Sybil looked perplexed as she studied the piece of paper, shaking her head.

"I had some signs; I thought they proved the message was from Grandpa. This must mean they weren't signs from Grandpa at all; they were just memories, like my dad said."

"Do not sound sad to have memories," The Great Sybil said. "Happy memories are treasures to be cherished. If you remember good times with your grandfather, you can be with him in your mind whenever you wish. That is better than waiting for a sign, over which you have no control."

Ellen stood up. "I'm going to find my parents," she said. "If they haven't found Corey yet, I'll tell them about this new message. Maybe they can get more meaning out of it than we can."

"I will come with you," The Great Sybil said. "They will have questions for me."

Ellen nodded. "Thank you."

The Great Sybil locked the trailer when they left. She and Ellen hurried together across the fairgrounds, toward the merry-go-round. As they approached The River of Fear ride, Ellen stopped.

"Corey wanted to go on The River of Fear," she said, "and it has a tunnel. There was an article about it in the paper and Corey kept talking about the Tunnel of Terror and how he couldn't wait to see what was in it."

"The ride is out of order," The Great Sybil said, pointing to the CLOSED sign which hung at the bottom of the steps to the platform. "They've had trouble with it all week."

Ellen looked at the darkened River of Fear. The loudspeaker that had boomed the spiel across the midway earlier, when she and Caitlin walked past, was silent.

"Maybe he was on it when it broke," Ellen said. "Maybe he got hurt."

"There's a first-aid building on the fairgrounds," The Great Sybil said. "Let's go there."

They walked away from The River of Fear.

CHAPTER

◈ 11 ◈

TUCKER KICKED The River of Fear control box. He did not like this plan. He did not like it one bit. It was easy for Mitch to tell him to stop the ride when the kid was inside the tunnel.

"Leave him in there until the fair closes," Mitch had said. "By the time you let him out, it won't matter how many cops he talks to. We'll be long gone."

"What about me?" Tucker said. "When he comes out, the kid will say I let you push him into the boat and the cops will start asking questions."

"Just say the ride malfunctioned. You lunged for the Off switch and I accidentally knocked the kid into the boat. Nobody can prove otherwise. All you have to do is act concerned and make a fuss over him. It'll be no problem. You'll end up looking like a hero for fixing the ride and rescuing the kid."

Tucker drank his coffee and looked at his watch. No problem. Ha. It was easy for Mitch to say, "No problem." He wasn't the one who would have to answer questions from the fair's security guards and the kid's parents and probably the cops and who knows how many others. Mitch and Joan would be off selling the loot and Tucker would be left to cover their tracks for them. He wasn't sure twenty percent of the profits was worth it. He suspected he wouldn't get the full twenty percent, either. He and Mitch might be brothers but there had never been a strong bond between them. Mitch had made that clear enough, when he refused to put up the bail last year when Tucker asked.

Tucker poured another half cup of coffee from his Thermos, sipping it sullenly. The kid was trouble. If he was smart enough to figure out Mitch and Joan's method of operation, he was smart enough to know that he was not knocked into the boat accidentally.

What if the kid said that Tucker threw him in the boat? What if his parents called the cops? What if the cops decided to run a check on Tucker and found out he was wanted in Oklahoma on that car insurance scam? What, then? Why should he risk going to jail while Mitch and Joan and that toady little Alan got off scot-free?

No! Tucker slammed his cup down on the control box so hard that coffee sloshed over the rim. No way was he going to take a chance on getting arrested again. He should never have tried to help Mitch in the first place but, now that he had, the only choice was to get rid of the kid.

He would turn the ride back on, right now, wait until the kid's boat came out, and let the kid get off.

He wouldn't say a word. He wouldn't pretend it had been an accident. He wouldn't lie and say the ride had malfunctioned.

He would help the kid out of the boat—and then the kid

would "accidentally" stumble and fall off the platform. The kid was short enough to go under the railing.

Tucker looked over the edge of the platform. There was no way a little kid could survive a fall from that height. It would be a horrible but completely believable accident. Lots of people stagger with dizziness when they get off The River of Fear ride; no one would doubt that the kid did, too.

Tucker himself would call for help. He would cry and go to pieces and tell how he tried to catch the kid before he went over the side. Tucker would give such a convincing performance that even the kid's parents would end up feeling sorry for him. And the kid would never tell them anything. Not ever again.

❖　❖　❖

COREY huddled in the bottom of the boat, waiting to see if it would start moving again. After a few moments, he sat up, keeping his hands in front of his face to protect himself from the slimy fake seaweed that now hung limply all around him.

With the eerie music and background noise silenced, and the boat standing still, it was easier to believe that it was only a ride and none of the evil creatures were real. Corey's courage returned.

He could think of two reasons why the ride had suddenly stopped: either it was broken again or else the man had deliberately stopped it while Corey was inside. The second explanation seemed most logical, since the man had forced Corey into the boat and pulled the switch before Corey could get out again.

The man wanted to get rid of me, Corey thought. The man

who ran The River of Fear ride was somehow connected with the thief. They threw me in here to keep me from telling the guards. Probably they plan to wait until the fair closes before they start the ride and let me off. By then, the thief would have stolen a million more wallets and purses and would be safely away from the fairgrounds.

I'll fool them, Corey thought. They think I'll just sit here in this boat and wait for the ride to start again. They think I'm a scaredy-cat baby who's afraid to do anything but wait. Well, I'm *not*! I'll get out and walk back through the Tunnel of Terror and climb out of The River of Fear ride and run past the man, down the steps, and call the police and tell them everything. They'll catch the thief and the ride operator and put them both in jail.

Corey put one hand over the side of the boat, easing his arm into the water. He leaned over, feeling for the bottom. It was concrete, and covered with algae but, as he had hoped, the water was only about eighteen inches deep. He could easily stand up in it.

Corey swung his legs over the side and stood up. The fake seaweed slapped at his cheeks. Water filled his shoes. Holding onto the side of the boat with one hand, he brushed at the seaweed with the other.

Since he wasn't sure how long the Tunnel of Terror was, he decided to walk back the way he had come. Gingerly, he took a step, holding one hand in front of him to feel what might be there. Corey's shoe slipped on the algae and as he tried to regain his balance, his foot splashed water, soaking his shirt. It was not going to be easy to walk.

He slid his feet forward, as if he were skiing, keeping one hand on the boat and one hand outstretched in front of his face. The tunnel was narrow, with barely enough room for him to move.

Slide, slide, slide. Three more steps. He passed the back of the boat and groped for the next boat in the line. Slide, slide. His left hand found a boat just as his right hand felt wet fur. Corey jerked his right hand back and then made himself reach out again. It must be the fake wolf. Corey inched closer, moving his hand across the wolf's body.

The animal blocked his way. He would have to climb over it, in order to continue, or else get in the boat beside him, crawl past the wolf, and then get back in the water. Corey put both hands on the wolf's huge back, and tried to pull himself up but his wet hands slipped on the fur and he couldn't get a good grip.

As he started to climb into the boat, the ride started up again.

The dim lights came on. Shrieks and screams filled the air. The wolf growled and lunged.

The boat zoomed forward, knocking Corey off balance. The wolf thrust its open jaws toward Corey, and Corey grabbed for the beast, to steady himself. His feet slid out from under him on the slippery wet floor and he fell backward, knocking his head against the side of the boat.

The last thing he saw before he lost consciousness was the wolf's jaws snapping closer and closer. Corey instinctively put an arm up, to protect his face. Then he closed his eyes and slithered downward toward the cold, black water.

❖ ❖ ❖

MR. AND Mrs. Streater returned to the fair office. The head of the security department told them an urgent message had been sent to all the security guards. One of them said he had talked to a small boy with a Batman bandage on his face when he responded to a report of a purse theft. According to his records, that had been at one P.M.

None of the guards had noticed Corey since then.

"It has been hectic all day," the woman in the office said. "We've had more thefts reported at the fair today than in all of the previous years combined. Today has been terrible! The security guards have been so busy that we called in extra help from the volunteer fire fighters."

"Something has happened to him," Mrs. Streater said. "I just know it."

"It's time to call the police," Mr. Streater said. "For all we know, Corey isn't on the fairgrounds any longer. He may have been kidnapped."

❖ ❖ ❖

AS ELLEN and The Great Sybil hurried toward the first-aid office, Ellen kept pondering the latest message. *The sign is untrue.* It sounded as if there had been only one sign, but she had thought there were several signs from Grandpa. Why didn't the message say, *The signs are untrue.*

Ellen stopped walking. "Sybil," she said, "what if that message meant a real sign? What if it meant an ordinary sign, with lettering, instead of a signal?"

"That's possible." The Great Sybil waved a hand in an arc, pointing at the booths and displays. "There are signs all around us."

"I wonder about the CLOSED sign," Ellen said slowly, "on The River of Fear. I keep thinking of that ride because of the word tunnel in the message. I just feel it's important."

90

"You should trust your feelings," The Great Sybil said.

"I'm going to go back there and talk to the man who operates the ride," Ellen said. "Maybe he knows something about Corey."

The Great Sybil nodded. "I'll inquire at the first-aid office," she said, "and then I'll return and meet you at The River of Fear."

Ellen turned and ran. The message mentioned a sign and a tunnel. The River of Fear ride had both. Maybe the ride had broken, as The Great Sybil thought, but instead of getting hurt, Corey was trapped inside. That would explain the part about darkness and not being able to see.

She knew that by now her parents were probably waiting for her at the merry-go-round, but it was important to talk to the man who ran The River of Fear ride as quickly as possible. He might not realize Corey was trapped. Probably all Ellen needed to do was tell the man her suspicions and he would help her find Corey. Mom and Dad would forgive her for taking so long when they learned that she had rescued her brother.

Ellen reached the CLOSED sign, stepped over the rope, and started up the wooden steps of The River of Fear. The lights on the ride blinked brightly and the spiel again boomed its message across the fairgrounds. The ride must be working again, although there were no other people on the steps. Ellen thought it was odd that the operator of the ride had forgotten to remove the CLOSED sign.

Above her on the platform, she saw the man who ran the ride. Hoping that he would be able to help her find Corey, Ellen climbed faster.

When she was almost to the top, the man saw her coming. "Go back down," he yelled. "This ride is closed."

Ellen continued to climb the steps.

The man met her at the top step. "Can't you read?" he said. "The ride is closed." He kept looking over his shoulder at the ride, as if expecting something to happen.

"I have to talk to you," Ellen said, "about my brother. I think he was on your ride when it broke down. I think he might still be in one of the boats."

The man's expression changed. Instead of looking annoyed at Ellen for ignoring his sign, he now appeared angry.

"Get out of here!" he yelled. "There wasn't any little kid on this ride."

He seemed furious with her. Ellen turned and started back down the steps. She had gone only two steps when she realized what the man had said. How did he know that her brother was a little kid? Ellen's brother might be a teenager or even an adult. Ellen had not mentioned Corey's age, yet the man instantly claimed there was no little kid on the ride.

Corey is, or was, on that ride, Ellen thought. Something happened to him, and the man knows it.

She went back to the top of the platform.

"My brother was on the ride when it broke," she said, "and I need to find him. Now."

The man turned and pulled a large lever. The River of Fear ride stopped. The sudden silence seemed ominous after the noise and lights.

"I told you to get off this platform," the man said. "If you don't leave right now, I will have you arrested for trespassing on private property."

"Where is Corey?"

"I already told you, I don't know anything about any little kid. When the ride broke, there were no people on it. Nobody. I realized in advance that there was a mechanical problem and I got everyone off safely."

"Corey's small. Maybe you missed him." Ellen peered around the man. The ride had stopped with one of the boats partially out of the opening through which they came at the end of the ride. "Maybe he's still in one of the boats. Why don't you start the ride again and let all of the boats come out?"

"No."

Ellen glared at the man. "Why not?" she demanded.

"I don't need to explain anything to you, girlie," he said, "but if you must know, I'm fixing a switch that isn't working right. It's probably going to take me the rest of the night so if you want to look in any of these boats, I suggest you come back tomorrow."

URGENT. The word flashed into Ellen's mind again. Urgent meant right now, not tomorrow. She wasn't sure what the man was trying to hide from her but she knew instinctively that he was not telling her the truth. She couldn't leave; not until she found Corey.

She lunged past the man and pushed the lever back up, starting The River of Fear ride again. If he wouldn't let the boats come out, she would do it herself.

The man grasped her shoulders, pulling her away from the control box. Ellen struggled briefly but quickly realized he was too strong for her. She quit fighting and said, "All right. I'll go. But I'll be back with my parents, and the police."

A look of fear flashed across the man's face and his fingers dug into her arms. "You should have left when I told you," he said. "Now you'll have to leave the hard way."

He shoved Ellen toward the side of the platform.

"Help!"

Ellen shouted as loudly as she could but with the spiel booming, she knew her voice would not be heard by anyone in the midway far below.

CHAPTER
◇ 12 ◇

THE Great Sybil was nearly to the first-aid office when she heard the voice inside her mind. "Help," it said. "Ellen needs help."

The Great Sybil stopped, feeling the gooseflesh rise on her arms, just as it used to do when she received her messages.

It had been so long, so terribly long, since she'd had a genuine message, that she was almost afraid to believe it was true.

Yet, she recognized the feeling instantly—the intuitive certain knowledge that what she was experiencing was a message from the spirits. The sensation was never there when she pretended to communicate. For all the years that she had postured and faked and bluffed, she had never once had this feeling of truth.

A thrill of gratitude ran through The Great Sybil. Her talent was back. She turned around immediately and raced toward The River of Fear.

◈ ◈ ◈

THE MAN pushed Ellen again, until her back was tight against the railing that surrounded the platform. Holding her arms against the railing, he kicked at her ankles, trying to knock her feet out from under her.

Ellen bent her head sideways and bit the man on the wrist, sinking her teeth in as far as she could. He gave a surprised cry of pain but did not let go of her.

As he kicked again at her ankles, Ellen raised her leg and aimed her knee at the man's groin.

He was too fast for her. He swore and jumped back, so that her knee barely touched his thigh. In doing so, he let go of Ellen's arms. She dodged his outstretched hand long enough to look at the line of boats which had now emerged at the end of the ride. They were empty.

The man's eyes followed her gaze and then, instead of grabbing for Ellen again, he stood and stared at the empty boats. Looking surprised, he pushed the lever to Off. This time, Ellen didn't try to stop him. She could see into all of the boats; Corey was not there.

"Are you satisfied now?" the man said. "I told you your brother was not on this ride. Now you can see for yourself. All the boats are here and there's no kid in any of them." He sounded relieved.

Ellen backed away from him, toward the steps. "You tried to kill me," she whispered.

"What?" The man laughed, as if that was the most outrageous statement ever made. "All I did was try to keep you

96

from pulling the lever that operates the ride when I was still working on the switch. You could have been electrocuted."

Ellen watched him warily, fearful that he would grab her again but the man acted as if their struggle had never happened. "You tried to push me over the side," she said.

"Your imagination is working overtime, girlie," he replied. "First you claim your brother is trapped on my ride and then you think I'm trying to kill you. You'd better quit watching so much TV and get yourself a real life."

Ellen glared at him. It was not, she knew, her imagination. The man had tried to push her over the edge of the platform, though she had no proof, no witnesses. The question was, why? Corey was *not* in one of the boats, as she had thought. The man apparently had nothing to hide, so it did not make sense for him to try to get rid of her.

Unless, she thought, he was just as surprised as Ellen when the boats were empty. Maybe he wanted Ellen gone because he didn't want her to be there when Corey came riding out in one of the boats. When Corey didn't come, the man no longer cared if Ellen saw the boats emerge.

The possibilities swished around in Ellen's mind like clothes in a washing machine but it was hard to think logically when she stood within six feet of someone who had just tried to kill her.

The man's change of attitude when he saw the empty boats could mean only one thing: he, too, had expected Corey to be in one of them. Since he wasn't, it meant Corey was still inside the ride.

Go into the darkness, the message said. *The smaller one sees not.*

Ellen said, "I want to go in the Tunnel of Terror."

97

"Sorry. The ride is closed until tomorrow."

"I don't want to go on the ride. I want to walk inside the tunnel. There must be a way to get in there, to fix anything that breaks."

"You don't give up easy, do you, girlie?"

Ellen backed away from him. She didn't want to make him angry again. Despite his denials, Ellen knew he had tried to push her off the platform. It wouldn't help Corey to have Ellen crumpled in a heap at the bottom of the platform while this creep pretended it was an accident.

"I'm going," Ellen said. Without waiting for a response, she turned and began to run down the wooden steps. She had gone less than halfway down when she saw The Great Sybil step over the CLOSED sign and start up the steps toward Ellen.

"Are you all right?" Sybil called.

Two against one, thought Ellen. With Sybil to help me, I'll get inside the tunnel.

"No! Corey's somewhere in the tunnel and the man on the platform tried to push me off."

Sybil stopped climbing as she listened.

"Hurry!" Ellen cried.

Ellen went back up the steps two at a time, with The Great Sybil on her heels. When they reached the top, they stopped. Ellen looked around, astonished.

The platform was empty.

"He must have gone in the tunnel himself," Ellen said. "He's gone after Corey." Quickly, Ellen told her what had happened.

"I have not trusted Tucker Garrenger from the first day I met him," The Great Sybil said. "When I look at Tucker, I see a black aura and I always sense feelings of guilt."

"We need to go in the tunnel after him," Ellen said. "He tried to push me off the platform; he might try to kill Corey, too."

"We must get help," The Great Sybil said. "This is not a task for us; we need the police. Hurry." She rushed back down the steps.

Ellen hesitated, knowing it would be sensible to follow The Great Sybil and then return with police or guards. But how long would that take? Five minutes? Ten? Too long. She couldn't leave Corey at the mercy of the evil Tucker all that time. She would go after Corey herself.

◈ ◈ ◈

OPPOSITE the platform, on the far side of the boats, a maintenance door led to a set of stairs on the back side of the ride. The painted face of the door was part of the huge picture of monsters that served as a sign for the ride.

Tucker stood behind the maintenance door, with the door slightly ajar. The girl was talking to The Great Sybil. Tucker frowned. How was the fortune-teller involved in this? Was she the girl's friend?

The idea of someone being able to see into the future or talk with spirits gave Tucker the creeps. Now, as he saw Sybil hurry away while the girl stayed on the platform, those psychic abilities alarmed him.

What if the girl had told The Great Sybil how Tucker tried to push her off the platform? For all he knew, Sybil could see into the past, as well as the future. She was probably on her way to get the cops; maybe she would tell them that Tucker was wanted in Oklahoma.

He knew the girl was going to go inside the ride to find her brother and by the time she came out with him, Sybil would be back here with the cops.

I can't stay at the fair, Tucker realized. The girl will accuse me of trying to push her off the platform and the boy will say Mitch and I threw him in the boat and I'll never be able to explain my way out of it. They'll run an ID check and I'll be slapped in jail. I'll have to leave with Mitch and Joan. They can drive me to Portland and I'll find another job there.

Tucker ran down the steps on the back side of The River of Fear and headed toward the parking lot. He hated to leave without collecting his pay from the fair but he'd have his share of the profits from Joan and Mitch. That would be enough to get him by for a few days.

Tucker ran up and down the rows of cars in the parking lot, his panic increasing until he spotted the Mercedes. The motor was running; Mitch was waiting for a chance to pull into the line of cars leaving the fairgrounds.

Tucker ran to the car and pounded on the door. "I'm going with you," he said. "We have to get out of here, fast."

"What happened?" Mitch said, as he reached behind him and unlocked the back door.

"The kid's big sister showed up and now she's gone off with a fortune-teller to tell the cops about us."

"Big sister?" Mitch said. "Fortune-teller?"

Tucker got in next to Alan and told them what had happened.

"You really botched it this time, Tucker," Joan snapped. "Why didn't you warn us that the boy was there? If you had done your job, none of this would have happened."

"How could I warn you?" Tucker said. "You told me to watch for a kid with a Batman bandage on his face, wearing a T-shirt with elephants on it. That kid didn't have either one."

Joan sniffed. "You never got anything right in your life," she said. She looked nervously around the parking lot, checking to be sure no one had followed Tucker.

"That boy can identify me," Mitch said slowly. "You told him my name." He sounded astonished, as if he could not believe his own words. He also sounded terrified.

"It will take them awhile to find the boy," Tucker said. "We can still get away, if we hurry."

"What do you mean, it will take awhile to find him?" Mitch said. "Isn't he with his sister? I thought you said she came to get him."

"She did but when the boats came out, they were empty. The little boy must have fallen out of the boat. No telling if he's alive or not."

"And the girl?"

"She went inside the ride to look for him."

"If the girl is inside the ride, looking for her brother," Mitch said, "maybe we can get to her before she talks to anyone." He pulled into a parking space and turned off the engine.

"What are you suggesting?" Joan said.

"It would look like they both fell off during the ride," Mitch said slowly. "A terrible accident."

"Mitch!" Joan said. "You can't kill those children just to avoid a pickpocket charge."

"It isn't the pickpocket charge he's worried about," Tucker said. "It's the other."

Joan's eyes narrowed to thin slits. "What other?" she said.

"You talk too much, Tucker," Mitch said.

"What other?" Joan repeated. "The charge against Tucker in Oklahoma?"

"I lurry," Mitch said, as he got out of the car. "We have to keep those kids from going to the cops."

"There are other ways to do that," Joan said, "besides murder."

"I know what I'm doing," Mitch said coldly, "and if you had not insisted on working the fair, it wouldn't be necessary."

"Can I go with you?" Alan said.

"May I go with you?" corrected Joan. "No, you may not. You stay in the car and if anyone asks you where your parents are, you say we're coming right back. Is that clear?" She opened the glove compartment and removed a flashlight.

Leaving Alan to pout on the back seat of the car, Joan and Mitch strode toward The River of Fear ride, with Joan insisting Mitch was making a mistake and Mitch ignoring her.

Tucker followed, glaring at their backs. Why didn't they ask him what he thought? Mitch and Joan always made him feel like a bumbling six year old with no brain.

CHAPTER
◇ 13 ◇

ELLEN WAS glad The Great Sybil was going for help; she had no doubt that it was needed. She was just as certain that she could not wait for it to arrive before she went after her brother.

Tucker's tool kit sat on the platform, next to the control box. Ellen opened it and removed a hammer. She wasn't eager to fight with anyone but if she needed to do so, she would have a weapon. Gripping it tightly in one hand, she stepped into the water of The River of Fear ride. She walked past the row of boats and into the enclosed ride where the boats immediately went over the edge of Whiplash Waterfall. Even with the ride turned off, she didn't see any way to go down the waterfall on foot. It was too steep and too slippery.

She returned to the boarding platform and then climbed into one of the boats and out the other side. To her left, she saw the outline of a door in the painted picture of monsters. She opened it and stepped through to the back side of the ride, the part the public never saw. As she had hoped, there was another set of steps. They were more like scaffolding than an actual stairway. There were also two landings, with doors that opened into the ride. Apparently, this was how maintenance was done.

She did not see the ride operator. Had he gone into the ride or had he run down these back stairs and left the area altogether? Maybe he had decided to make his escape before Ellen could go to the police.

Quickly, Ellen climbed down the scaffolding to the first door, which was less than a third of the way down. It probably opened to the middle of the waterfall part of the ride. Since the message specified the tunnel, Ellen continued down the steps to the lower door.

Putting her hand on the knob, she turned it as quietly as she could and pushed the door open. A dank, rotten odor drifted out of the darkness. Ellen put her hand over her nose and mouth, not wanting to inhale it. What was she getting into, anyway? Maybe she should wait for The Great Sybil to return with help.

Ellen peered into the blackness, blinking to adjust her eyes. Was Corey somewhere in that foul-smelling hole, in need of help?

She stood still, listening. If the man was in here, she thought she would be able to hear movement. She heard nothing. Quickly, before she could change her mind, she stepped inside, onto a walkway that extended into the ride. Noiselessly, she closed the door behind her so that if the man was still outside, he would not realize where she was.

It was completely dark and silent. Too silent. If Corey was trapped inside this tunnel, surely he would be calling for help. Unless, she thought, he's unable to.

The odor was worse with the door closed. Ellen kept one

hand over her face. The other hand, which held the hammer, she extended out in front of her. She took a step forward.

She wanted to call out for Corey but if Tucker was in here, she didn't want him to know where she was.

She took another step and another—and walked off into air. The walkway had ended. As she flailed her arms, grasping for something to break her fall, she dropped the hammer. She plunged down, landing in cold water that came partway up her leg. The hammer splashed somewhere in front of her.

Ellen stood in the water, feeling behind her for the walkway. It hit her at shoulder height. She bent her knees, testing her legs for injury. Although the fall had scared her half to death, she was not hurt.

If Tucker was in here he would have heard the splash as she fell; he would have no trouble finding her. She listened, turning her head, but still she heard nothing, no indication that anyone else was near.

The concrete floor under the water was slick and she realized that the damp, moldy smell which filled her nostrils originated under the water. It's like walking through the sewers, she thought, and shuddered.

She believed she was in the middle of the ride, where the boats go through the tunnel. If Corey had come into The River of Fear at the beginning and not come out at the end, he had to be somewhere in this darkness.

She moved forward carefully, feeling with one foot before she inched her body forward.

She went a few more feet and bumped smack into a huge, furry beast. Stifling a scream, Ellen stood perfectly still, waiting to see if the beast was real. Her brain told her: of course it is not real, it's only a prop for the ride. Although she believed her brain, she could not keep her heart from pounding wildly as she tentatively put out a hand and felt the creature's coarse fur.

It was a bear or a wolf or some other large wild animal. It did not move at her touch and she told herself again that it was only a fake. She moved her hands along the animal's back, toward its neck. When she reached the head, her fingers touched flesh. Warm, human flesh.

She jerked her hand away and, for one brief instant, swayed dizzily. It would have been a relief to faint. Instead, she clenched her teeth tightly together, took a deep breath, and reached out again. She had touched a human arm. She forced her hands to keep moving. A body lay on its stomach across the animal's enormous head, one hand on the beast's back, the other hand dangling.

The person, Ellen knew, was not part of The River of Fear ride. Fake bodies are not warm.

Like a blind person reading Braille, Ellen moved her fingertips across the body's narrow shoulders. It was a child. Corey? Ellen's breath came faster. There was a lump on the side of the head, as if someone—or something—had struck the person with a heavy object.

"Corey?" she whispered. "Is that you?"

She moved her hands more slowly as she reached for the body's face. It was easier to feel a shirt than bare skin. Her fingers inched carefully across an ear, toward the cheek.

Ellen froze for an instant and then patted the face frantically, feeling as quickly as she could. The Batman bandage was gone, but the scab of Corey's cut still slashed diagonally from cheekbone to chin.

"Corey!" she said. "Wake up!"

There was no reply.

Ellen slid her hand between Corey's chest and the back of the breast, feeling for a heartbeat. Before she knew who the person was, her touch had been tentative; now, her hands pressed firmly against her brother's T-shirt.

Was he breathing? She couldn't find a heartbeat. Remembering how her mother always took her own pulse when she was exercising by feeling the sides of her throat, Ellen quickly put her hands on Corey's neck.

Tears of relief stung Ellen's eyes as life throbbed beneath her fingers. He was alive. He was unconscious but at least he was alive.

She dipped her hands in the cold water and patted it on Corey's neck, slapping him lightly to try to rouse him. He groaned but did not wake up.

Ellen grabbed Corey's limp arms and pulled. "Stand up," she said, but Corey seemed stuffed with cotton. She would have to get him on her back and carry him.

She put her hands under Corey's arms, held tight, and lifted. He slid toward her, across the back of the beast. His feet splashed into the water, touched the bottom, and kept on sliding. Ellen staggered backward in the water, trying to keep her balance.

"Wake up, Corey," she pleaded. She had hoped to maneuver him onto her back and carry him out but in his unconscious state, he seemed to weigh two hundred pounds.

"Ohhh," said Corey.

Keeping her hands clasped tightly around his chest, to keep him from sliding further into the water, she tried to shake him. "Wake up!" she repeated.

Corey groaned again.

She tried to hoist him upward, across her shoulder, but he was too heavy.

I can't carry him, Ellen realized. I'll have to drag him out of here.

Still clutching Corey around the chest, she began to walk backwards through the tunnel. Corey's head hung down, with his chin on his chest; his feet trailed behind him in the water. She wondered how Corey got the lump on his head. Who hit him? How much damage was done?

Suddenly, Ellen remembered reading that an injured person who was unconscious should not be moved until a doctor arrived because there might be a spinal cord injury. It was possible to break the person's neck and cause permanent paralysis. Visions of Corey in a wheelchair flashed across her mind.

What have I done? she wondered. I should have left him where he was and gone for help. Well, it was too late now. She sloshed backwards, dragging the limp Corey with her.

Her arms ached and it was all she could do to hold onto him. Thank goodness the door she had come through was not too far. Her shoe slipped on the algae and she could not put her arms out to regain her balance. She sat down, hard, in the water.

She scrambled quickly to her feet and stood for a moment, with Corey's wet body pressed against her chest, letting the pain in her rear end subside. She was soaked and scared and sorry she had come into the tunnel alone. The man who ran the ride must not have come inside the tunnel looking for Corey, after all. If he had, he surely would have heard her splashing around and talking to Corey.

Well, she told herself, it won't do any good to stand here and cry. I have to get Corey to a doctor.

Mentally, she repeated part of her favorite childhood story: "I think I can, I think I can, I think I can."

She started moving again, toward the walkway by the door. She would not let herself wonder how she was going to get Corey up on the walkway when she reached it.

CHAPTER

❖ 14 ❖

WHEN MITCH and Joan, with Tucker on their heels, reached The River of Fear, the midway around it was empty.

"It's almost time for the fair to close," Tucker said.

"Maybe they're still inside," Mitch said. "Both of them."

He went around to the back side of the ride, to the bottom of the maintenance stairs. Joan followed. "I still don't think we should do this," Joan said.

"You're the one who wanted to work the fair."

"I wanted to lift a few wallets. I didn't want to kill any children."

"You don't have to."

Mitch climbed to the lower of the two doors. Joan hesitated and then climbed after him.

"If anyone comes," she told Tucker, "start the spiel."

Tucker did not answer. Why should he stand guard for them while they did this? There wasn't anything in it for him. He would be guilty of helping them and he wasn't sure they would get away with it. One kid falling off the platform was believable; a pair of kids falling off the ride was too unlikely. The cops were sure to be suspicious. And what about the fortuneteller? How much did she know?

A new plan hatched in Tucker's mind. He would wait until Joan and Mitch were way inside the ride. Then he would turn it on, send the boats whizzing through, and make Joan and Mitch fear for their lives.

He would leave Joan and Mitch in the ride and drive the Mercedes away from the fair himself. He would sell the valuables they had stolen, take the cash, and deliver the car to the stripper. That would show Joan and Mitch who was an idiot and who wasn't. If Alan had a fit, well, Tucker could always abandon him on some country road.

Tucker went around to the front of The River of Fear and climbed the steps to the platform. Smiling at his own cleverness, he stood beside the On/Off lever and waited. He wanted to be sure Mitch and Joan were far from the door, deep in the Tunnel of Terror, before he turned the ride on and left.

◈ ◈ ◈

THE Great Sybil burst through the door of the fair office.

"There are two children in danger," she panted.

A security guard, who had been pouring himself a cup of coffee to celebrate the fact that the fair was now closed for the night, put the cup down and snapped to attention. "Where?" he said.

"The River of Fear ride. They need help."

"Who are they?" the guard asked.

"Ellen and Corey Streater. Ellen almost got killed once and now she needs help again."

"Corey?" The guard reached for the two-way radio that hung from his belt. "Corey Streater?"

"That's correct," The Great Sybil said.

"That's the kid who is missing." The guard spoke into the radio. "All security personnel to The River of Fear ride," he said. "Fast. And have the Sheriff set up a roadblock. Check all cars before they leave the fairgrounds."

He ran out the office door; The Great Sybil ran after him. As the last of the fair patrons straggled out the gates, every guard on the grounds rushed toward The River of Fear.

❖ ❖ ❖

MR. AND Mrs. Streater stood next to the merry-go-round, watching as the attendants locked the ride.

"Ellen should have been here by now," Mrs. Streater said. "It doesn't take this long to look in the sheep barn."

Two guards ran past. Mr. and Mrs. Streater looked at each other and, without saying a word, ran after the guards.

❖ ❖ ❖

ELLEN staggered backwards through the slimy water until she reached the walkway. She looked up toward where she thought the door through which she had entered The River of Fear was. It might as well be a mile away, she thought. The edge of the walkway was shoulder high and there was no way she could lift Corey's inert body that far. She stood in the water, her aching arms holding her unconscious brother.

"Help!" she called. "In here! Help!"

To her astonishment, the door above her opened. Although she had hoped someone might hear her, she never dreamed anyone would happen to be close enough the first time she called for help.

"Down here!" Ellen cried. "I'm down here in the water."

A flashlight beamed downward; Ellen shut her eyes and turned her head away from the sudden light.

"It's both of them," said a woman. "The girl and the boy."

"Stay where you are," a man called. "We're coming to get you."

Tears of relief sprang to Ellen's eyes. These people must have been looking for her and Corey, and just happened to be close to the maintenance door when Ellen called out.

Splash! Someone jumped over the edge of the landing, dropping into the water beside Ellen and Corey. The flashlight still shone down from above. Ellen smiled gratefully at her rescuer, a dark-haired man in a dark blue shirt. "Corey's hurt," she said. "You'd better get him out first and come back for me."

The man did not reply.

Ellen's smile faded when she saw the way he looked at her. His eyes seemed cold, like steel marbles. His jaws were clenched and a muscle twitched rhythmically in one cheek as he moved toward her. With horror, Ellen realized he had not come to rescue them.

"Who are you?" she whispered. "What do you want?"

He put his hands on her shoulders, pushing her backwards. Ellen twisted, trying to get away.

She couldn't hold Corey up out of the water and fight off an attacker at the same time. If she let go of Corey and tried to escape, Corey would surely drown. If she didn't drop Corey, they were both going to drown.

Ellen screamed.

Whoever was holding the flashlight quickly shut the door.

❖   ❖   ❖

THE Great Sybil and the guard ran toward The River of Fear as other guards and police officers converged from all directions.

"The ride is closed," the guard said. "There's no one there."

"Go inside," The Great Sybil said. "They're in the tunnel."

"Are you sure?" said a second guard.

"We've looked everywhere for that boy," said a third guard. "We may as well check inside The River of Fear ride, too."

"Hurry!" Sybil implored.

As the guard ran toward the wooden steps to the platform, Tucker stood at the top, waiting for Joan and Mitch to get deep in the ride and dreaming about what he would do with his unexpected windfall. Intent on his plan to get even, he did not notice the guards hurrying toward him. He smiled, pulled the lever, and started the ride.

Inside the ride, the dim lights came on and the sound effects boomed into the darkness. Ellen stared at her attacker's face as she struggled to get away from him. The unexpected noise of the ride starting caused him to loosen his grip temporarily but, burdened as she was with Corey's limp body, Ellen could not move quickly enough to take advantage of the man's distraction.

Now he shoved Ellen again, trying to push her under the water. She staggered backwards, desperately trying to keep her balance.

Behind him, Ellen saw a boat enter the tunnel and come toward them.

The man yelled, "Joan! Tell Tucker to turn this thing off! What's he trying to do, kill us all?"

"Maybe he's trying to warn us that someone is coming."

The flashlight went off.

With the man momentarily inattentive, Ellen thought: This is my chance. As soon as the boat was close enough, she heaved Corey upward with all her might and dropped him over the side, into the bottom of the boat. She hoped she was not making Corey's injuries worse by dumping him into the boat that way but the alternative, drowning, was even worse.

The next boat approached; Ellen grabbed hold and swung one leg over the side. As her second foot came out of the water, the man's arms went around her waist and pulled with such force that Ellen was yanked backwards away from the boat.

"The boy's gone!" Mitch said. "He's in one of the boats."

Ellen kicked furiously and, twisting out of his grasp, dropped to her hands and knees on the slimy bottom.

"Joan! Get down here and help me," Mitch said. "She's slippery as a bar of soap."

As he grabbed for her, Ellen ducked away from him and crawled under the walkway.

Joan tiptoed out the door. Instead of telling Tucker to turn the ride off, she hurried down the back steps, and ran toward the car. Mitch was going to drown that girl just to keep the cops away from Tucker. And if she stayed here, she'd be an accomplice.

Picking a few pockets had been fun, and stealing cars and parting them out was lucrative. But Joan drew the line at murder. Especially a kid. She had never seen Mitch act this way. He liked kids. He'd always been good to Alan. That's one reason Joan had married him; she knew Alan needed a man in his life. But Alan did not need a man who was wanted for murder.

When Joan didn't answer him, Mitch dropped to his knees in the filthy water and began reaching under the platform.

"I know you're under there," he said.

CHAPTER
· 15 ·

TUCKER KEPT his hand on the lever for a few seconds after he pulled it, imagining the scene inside the ride. As he turned to leave, Joan dashed from behind The River of Fear and started across the midway. Tucker stared down at her, confused. Where was she going? Where was Mitch? Why didn't she signal to Tucker?

The two of them were cutting him out! The thought hit him like a snowball striking the back of his neck, sending shivers of shock down his spine. It was the only logical explanation why Joan would run away like that. Mitch must be ahead of her. Joan and Mitch did the dirty work and then, instead of coming up the platform for Tucker, they beat it back to their fancy-dancy Mercedes and left Tucker to take the rap.

Well, he would not let them get away with it. The fact that *he* had planned to cut *them* out did not lessen Tucker's outrage as he rushed down the steps, arriving at the bottom just as three patrol cars pulled up. Two officers got out of each car.

For a moment, Tucker stood frozen with fright. Then he said, "The ride has malfunctioned. It won't stop until I go to the main electrical center and trip the fuse." To his vast relief, the officers did not detain him.

Tucker broke into a trot, headed for the parking lot and the Mercedes. He had to get there before Mitch and Joan drove off.

They tricked me, Tucker thought bitterly, as he ran. They got me to stand guard and then they left me to face the cops alone.

An ambulance sped past, its red lights whirling.

Each time his feet hit the pavement, Tucker grew more furious. His own brother had cut him out.

At the far end of the parking lot, a line of cars waited to exit. There, almost at the end of the line, was the Mercedes, with Joan behind the wheel. Tucker pounded on the locked door until Joan rolled down her window.

"Let me in," Tucker said.

"What do you want?"

"I'm going with you. I want my cut." He reached through Joan's open window, unlocked the back door, and climbed into the back seat. Then he saw that Alan sat in front with Joan and the back seat was empty.

"Where's Mitch?" he asked.

"He's meeting us later," Joan said.

Tucker stared at the back of Joan's head. "You left him, didn't you?" he said, unable to keep the amazement out of his voice. "You left your own husband to take the rap."

"Shut up, Tucker. There won't be any cuts for any of us if we don't get out of here soon. This traffic is terrible."

"What if the cops find him?"

"Mitch can talk his way out of anything. He'll catch up to us in Portland."

"You can't let the cops take Mitch in," Tucker said. "What if they fingerprint him?"

"What if they do? Mitch doesn't have a record."

"He never told you?"

Joan swiveled around so she could see Tucker's face. "Told me what?"

"Nothing," Tucker said. "Forget I said that."

"Told me *what*?"

Tucker wiped the perspiration off his brow and looked out the window. "I thought you knew," he said. "I just assumed Mitch had told you."

"Tucker!" Her voice hissed, like a poisonous snake. "If you don't tell me, right now, what you are talking about, I will turn you in to the cops."

Tucker pointed at the back of Alan's head.

"Alan," Joan said, "get out and go see if you can figure out why traffic isn't moving."

"I want to hear about Mitch."

"Go!"

Alan opened the car door and walked off.

"Ten years ago," Tucker said, "Mitch was convicted of armed robbery and assault. After the trial, while he was being transferred from the county jail to a state prison, he escaped; he got away from two guards and was never caught. He lost thirty pounds, had plastic surgery on his nose, cut his hair short, and changed his name."

"His name?" Joan said. "Mitch Lagrange is not his real name?"

"No. His real name is Michael Garrenger."

"I married someone called Mitch Lagrange."

Tucker was sorry he had spilled his brother's secret but it was almost worth it to hear the shock in Joan's voice.

Alan rushed back to the car. "You know why we're going so slow?" he said. "It's because there are cops up ahead, and they're checking every car."

❖ ❖ ❖

ELLEN heard splashing as the man moved beside the edge of the walkway. She couldn't see his face but she sensed that he was peering under the walkway every few feet, trying to see where she was.

The thick algae squished up between her fingers as she crawled through the water. The foul smell was worse under the walkway, where the water was more stagnant. She wondered if the smell was part of the scary effect of The River of Fear or merely the result of poor maintenance.

This water is probably full of germs, she thought, and gagged at the idea of crawling on her hands and knees through zillions of wriggling creatures, all carrying terrible diseases.

She heard another row of empty boats enter the tunnel. They moved quickly, so there was no time to form a plan or consider where the man was standing. As the boats went past, Ellen sprang out from under the walkway, grabbed the side of a boat and jumped headfirst into the bottom of the boat.

She almost made it. She landed in the bottom of the boat but couldn't get her legs tucked in fast enough. The man grasped her ankles and tugged. Ellen kicked, trying to free herself. The man ran along beside the moving boat, yanking on her legs.

Ellen grabbed the safety bar but her hands were slippery

from crawling around in the algae and when the man tugged harder, she was unable to keep her grip. He pulled her up and over the edge. Although she tried desperately to cling to the side of the boat, it slid away from her outstretched fingers.

The man held fast to her ankles and Ellen fell face downward into the water. Immediately, she felt a foot on her shoulders, holding her under.

CHAPTER
◦ 16 ◦

ELLEN TWISTED and kicked. The foot moved off her shoulders but now the man's hands pressed hard on the back of her head. Ellen felt as if her lungs would burst like popped balloons if she didn't get some air soon.

Help! she screamed in her mind. Grandpa! Guardian Angel! Spirits! Anyone! Help me!

But even as she pleaded, Ellen knew that she would have to help herself.

Empty boats streaked past beside her, so close, yet so unreachable.

Frantically, Ellen scooped a fistful of algae from the bottom and flung it over her shoulder at the man. He was leaning over her, holding her head down. The foul-smelling algae hit him in both eyes, temporarily blinding him.

Cursing, he let go of Ellen in order to wipe the algae from his face. She scrambled to her feet, gulped air, and dove into the last boat in the row.

As she rode away from him, she heard him yell, "Joan! Where are you? Turn on the light!"

A short distance ahead, the wolf lunged low toward the side of the boat, then raised its head as the boat passed, snapping its huge jaws.

Ellen realized that when Corey had been knocked unconscious, the wolf's head must have come along just at the right moment to lift Corey and raise his limp body up, keeping him out of the water. When the ride stopped, Corey still lay on the wolf's head. If the wolf had not been there, Corey would surely have drowned in the foul water.

Her boat passed the enormous beast. Instead of being scared of the vicious-looking creature, Ellen felt like hugging it.

She continued on through the Tunnel of Terror and past all the horrible monsters of Mutilation Mountain. Under ordinary circumstances, she would have been scared silly by the Dracula, werewolf, and other horrid creatures. This time, she barely noticed them. She was too shaken by her encounters with real danger to be frightened by anything fake.

After what seemed like an hour, she emerged at the top of The River of Fear platform. It was crowded with people.

"There she is! Ellen's here!"

Ellen recognized The Great Sybil's voice.

Below, the red lights of an ambulance flashed around and around near the bottom of the steps.

A police officer and The Great Sybil helped Ellen climb out of the boat. The officer turned the ride off.

"Corey's in one of the other boats," Ellen said. "He's unconscious."

"We already found him," the officer said. "A paramedic is

examining him now." He called over the side of the platform. "Mrs. Streater! Mr. Streater! Your daughter is safe!"

Below her, Ellen saw her parents standing next to two men in white jackets. Corey lay on a stretcher beside them.

Her parents waved at her and then bent over Corey again.

"What happened?" The Great Sybil said.

"A man inside The River of Fear tried to kill me," Ellen said. She started to shake. Her teeth chattered as if it were a freezing December night instead of a balmy August evening.

"Here." The Great Sybil removed the fringed shawl that she had on and wrapped it around Ellen's shoulders.

"I'm not really cold," Ellen said. "I don't know why I'm shivering."

"Nervous reaction," said the police officer. "Who tried to kill you? How?"

The officer raised his eyebrows but listened intently as Ellen told exactly what had happened inside The River of Fear ride. Partway through her story, he directed two other officers to look for suspects on the maintenance stairway on the back side of the ride.

"It was Tucker Garrenger," The Great Sybil said. "He's the only one who would know to go inside the ride." She frowned. "I can't think who the woman would be, though."

"Who is Tucker Garrenger?" the officer said.

"He's been running this ride," The Great Sybil said, "and I haven't trusted him from the very first."

"The man inside wasn't the man who was running the ride," Ellen said. "The man who tried to drown me wasn't the same man who tried to push me off the platform."

"*Two* men tried to kill you?" the officer said.

Ellen nodded. She didn't blame the officer for looking dubious; she could hardly believe it herself.

"The man in the water," Ellen said, "was average height and build and he had thick, dark hair. And evil eyes." She shivered harder, remembering how the man had looked at her. "And he kept talking to someone named Joan."

The siren on the ambulance bleeped. Ellen jumped at the sudden sound and then quickly looked down. The medics were sliding the stretcher bearing Corey into the ambulance.

Corey lay still as stone. Mrs. Streater climbed in the back of the ambulance and knelt beside Corey. Mr. Streater looked up, waved at Ellen, and pointed to the ambulance before he, too, climbed in.

Ellen waved back. Her parents were going to accompany Corey to the hospital. It must be serious, for both of them to go, leaving her here. Even though they could see that she was unharmed and did not need their assistance, it was unlike her parents to take off like that without explaining to her first.

And what about the Streaters' car? Dad must be in a terrific hurry to get to that hospital, if he was leaving his car at the fairgrounds, to be retrieved later.

Ellen knew that the police officers or The Great Sybil would be sure that Ellen got safely home. Maybe Dad had arranged for the police to drive Ellen to the hospital when they finished questioning her. Even so, she trembled harder as she watched both of her parents and her brother leave the fairgrounds in an ambulance, its siren wailing and its red lights flashing. Surrounded by people, Ellen felt completely alone.

CHAPTER
◦ 17 ◦

MITCH SPAT into the water and wiped more algae from his face. "They got away," he muttered. "Both of them."

The only sound was the splash of the boats in the distance and the noises of the scenes in the tunnel.

Mitch sloshed through the foul-smelling water toward the landing. Joan had said maybe someone was coming. She must have slipped outside to watch and listen. Or maybe she had gone back up the steps to tell that idiot Tucker to turn the ride off. Mitch could not imagine what had possessed Tucker to turn the thing on in the first place. Tucker knew Mitch and Joan were inside; what was he thinking?

Furious, Mitch hoisted himself onto the landing and pushed open the door. "Joan?" he whispered.

Where was she?

He heard voices now, excited voices. A loud babble came from the front side of The River of Fear. He had to get out of there before the girl talked to anyone.

"Joan?"

If she had climbed up to tell Tucker to turn the ride off, she would be on the front side of the ride by now. Surely, if the voices were guards or cops, Joan would hightail it back to warn him. Unless she couldn't. Maybe Joan had no choice but to talk to them, too. She'd figure out some lie, some way to throw them off the track until Mitch got away. He just hoped that idiot, Tucker, kept his mouth shut and let Joan do the talking.

Silently, keeping as close to the back side of the ride as he could, Mitch glided down the maintenance steps. When his feet were on solid ground, he looked around carefully, still hoping to find Joan waiting for him. He didn't like going to the car without her. He decided to wait a few minutes, just in case she returned.

There were more voices now and lights shone over the top of The River of Fear. Mitch chewed on his lip and wished he could light up a cigarette.

A siren shrieked. Mitch jumped at the sudden, close sound. Sirens, any kind of sirens, were bad news. He could wait no longer. Joan had probably gone back to the car and was waiting for him there.

Mitch hurried through the darkness, away from the back of The River of Fear. His mind raced ahead to what he would do if Joan was *not* waiting in the car. Should he take Alan and leave, trusting Joan would contact him through their man in Portland? Or maybe her mother. Joan could always go to her mother's place, knowing Mitch would eventually come for her there.

He concentrated so hard on his own thoughts that he did not hear the footsteps behind him. When the police officer spoke, Mitch tried to run but by then it was too late. A second officer quickly cut him off.

"We'd like to talk to you," one officer said.

Mitch silently cursed himself for hanging around so long, waiting for Joan.

"How did you get so wet?" the older officer, Sergeant Hall, said. "Your clothes are soaked, clear to your waist."

"Some kid spilled his Coke on me. I tried to wash it out in the rest room."

"Sure."

Mitch said, "I'm a hard working, law-abiding citizen and if you don't have anything better to do than harass me, I suggest you let me be on my way before I file suit for unlawful arrest."

The two officers exchanged a glance. "Something doesn't add up," Sergeant Hall said. "Why would he try to kill some girl he doesn't know? What is he hiding?"

"I'm not hiding anything," Mitch said, "and I certainly did not try to kill anyone."

"I want a fingerprint check," Sergeant Hall said.

"I want a lawyer," Mitch replied.

The younger officer began to read Mitch his rights.

❖ ❖ ❖

ELLEN RODE in the back seat of the police car, with Sybil beside her. She felt disconnected from reality, as if she were watching herself in a home video. People in the cars they passed peered curiously in the window at her, no doubt wondering what crime she had committed. If Ellen had not been so worried about Corey, she would have enjoyed the adventure.

The police car pulled into the hospital's emergency entrance and dropped Ellen and Sybil off. The admitting clerk gave them directions to a family waiting area. When they got there, it was empty. Ellen paced nervously until, a few minutes later, Mrs. Streater came in. She hugged Ellen and said, "They're X-raying Corey now. He's still unconscious."

Ellen introduced The Great Sybil to her mother.

"I'm going in to stay with Corey," Mrs. Streater said. "I'll come back as soon as I know anything."

A nurse stopped to tell them there was free coffee, tea, or cocoa in the small kitchen adjoining the waiting area. After Ellen got a cup of cocoa and The Great Sybil fixed some tea, they returned to the waiting room.

"I've finally quit shaking," Ellen said.

"You had a terrible scare."

"If you had not helped me get the last message about the sign and the tunnel," Ellen said, "we would not have found Corey in time. How can I ever thank you?"

"You already have. Because of you, my psychic gifts have been returned to me."

"Me?" Ellen said. "What did I do?"

"You made me care enough to try to help with no thought of benefit for myself." She told Ellen how she received the word *help* as a message.

"Who sent it?" Ellen asked.

The Great Sybil smiled and shrugged. "Maybe the same spirit who sent your messages."

"I wish I knew who that was," Ellen said. "Without the messages, we would never have thought to look for Corey in The River of Fear. Who helped us?"

"Who helped us? Your grandfather? God? A guardian angel? Who knows?" The Great Sybil sipped her tea and gazed out the window. "Some questions have no answers," she said. "They only have possibilities."

"I'd like to believe my messages were from Grandpa," Ellen said, "but since there's no way to prove it, I'm not going to try to get any more messages. I have my memories of Grandpa and that is enough."

"You are wise, just as your name implies."

Mr. Streater hurried into the waiting room. "Corey's awake," he said. "He woke up as he was leaving the X-ray room."

Feeling giddy with relief, Ellen hugged her father. Then, for good measure, she hugged The Great Sybil, too.

"There's something wrong with his voice," Mr. Streater said, "but the doctors don't think it's related to the bump on his head. They're getting Corey settled in a room now; you can see him in a few minutes."

The Great Sybil said she would stay in the waiting room but Ellen insisted that she go in to see Corey, too. "If it weren't for you," she said, "Corey might not be alive."

They found Corey lying in bed, sucking on lemon throat lozenges.

"He has a concussion," Mrs. Streater said, "but the doctors think there will be no lasting problems."

"What about his voice?" Ellen asked.

"He screamed too much at the fair," Mrs. Streater said.

Laughter bubbled out of Ellen as she looked at Corey.

The police officer who had driven Ellen and The Great Sybil to the hospital came into Corey's room. "I thought you would like to know that Tucker Garrenger was picked up when he tried to leave the fairgrounds with a woman driving a stolen

Mercedes. It turns out he was wanted in Oklahoma on an insurance fraud charge."

"I'm not surprised," The Great Sybil said. "He had guilt written all over him."

"We suspect the woman, Joan Lagrange, and her husband are responsible for a string of car thefts in recent weeks, both in Seattle and Vancouver, British Columbia."

"What about the man who tried to drown me?" Ellen asked.

"That was Joan's husband, Mitch. We caught him behind The River of Fear ride. His real name is Michael Garrenger; he's Tucker's brother. When we put his fingerprints into the system, we learned the F.B.I. has been looking for him for years."

"I knew it!" rasped Corey. "I told the guard that the man with the shopping bag was wanted by the F.B.I. I bet that woman whose purse he took was really a movie actress in disguise, too."

"Hush, Corey," Mrs. Streater said. "Save your voice."

"So they tried to kill Ellen to avoid being questioned by the police," The Great Sybil said.

"What about the things they stole?" Corey said. "The purse and the wallets?" The throat lozenges were helping; he could actually be understood.

"It was all in the trunk of the car," the officer said. "We found cameras, purses, even a cellular telephone. There were shopping bags full of stolen goods."

"White shopping bags," squeaked Corey triumphantly, "with blue and red lettering on the side, just like I said." He coughed and put another lozenge in his mouth.

"Joan's nine-year-old son helped them pick pockets," the officer said. "He dropped his ice cream, to distract the victims."

The officer shook his head sadly. "He'll go into a foster home now. I hope it isn't too late to straighten him out."

A doctor came in to check Corey.

"When can I go home?" Corey asked.

"It's a little early to say," the doctor said. "Probably a day or two."

"I have to leave tomorrow morning," Corey said, "while the fair is still on."

"Surely you don't want to go back to the fair, after all that happened," The Great Sybil said.

"I have to spy on the bottle-booth man," Corey said. "He is cheating."

"This family," said Mrs. Streater, "will be the death of me."

"You've done quite enough spying," said Mr. Streater. "You'll have to wait until next year to go to the fair again."

"Will you be back next year?" Ellen asked The Great Sybil.

The Great Sybil shook her head. "The Great Sybil is retiring. From now on, I'm just plain Sybil."

"No more contacting the spirits?" Ellen asked.

"No. At least, not for money."

"Next year," whispered Corey, "I'm going to ride The River of Fear before I ride the roller coaster, so I can be sure to scream loud."

"Next year," said Mrs. Streater firmly, "you are going to the fair with us and we are staying far away from The River of Fear."

"But I never got to see the monsters of Mutilation Mountain," Corey said.

"They were stupid," said Ellen. "Just a bunch of werewolves and Dracula look-alikes."

"*You* went on The River of Fear?" In his astonishment,

Corey started to sit up, then groaned and lay back down again.

"I didn't have much choice," Ellen said.

"Were you scared?"

Ellen thought about the fake monsters and started to say, *no*. Then she remembered the face of Mitch Lagrange as he shoved her backwards into the dark water.

"I was scared," she said. "I was absolutely terrified."

Corey smiled happily. "I can hardly wait for next year," he said.

EPILOGUE

THE HALL clock chimed once.

One o'clock in the morning. Ellen was astonished to realize she had whispered into the darkness for a whole hour. In all that time, she had never had any reason to think that Grandpa's spirit heard her, yet she felt serene for the first time since the day of the accident.

"Thanks for listening, Grandpa," Ellen said. "I miss you and love you. I always will."

She opened her hand, feeling in the dark for the ends of the silver chain. Holding one end in each hand, she reached behind her neck and fastened the clasp.

She slid back into bed, letting the silver elephant remain on the outside of her nightgown.

Her anger that Grandpa had been cruelly snatched away, his life snuffed out like a heel grinding a match, was gone. In its place was the belief that Grandpa had merely crossed an invisible line into a new state of being.

Ellen could not begin to imagine where he was or how he looked. Oddly, it didn't matter. As Sybil said, some questions don't have answers. They only have possibilities.

Peg Kehret's books for young readers are regularly recommended by the American Library Association and the International Reading Association. She has won numerous state awards, as well as the Golden Kite Award from the Society of Children's Book Writers and Illustrators and the PEN Award for Children's Literature.

Ms. Kehret and her husband live in a log house near Mount Rainier National Park in Washington State. From her home office she watches deer, elk, hummingbirds, and hawks. The couple have two grown children, four grandchildren, a dog, and two cats. When she is not writing, Ms. Kehret likes to read, watch baseball, and pump her old player piano.